BROWN DAY

Daniel J. Travanti

CONTENTS

Foreword

To Whom it may concern

I have written these short stories over a period of forty-two years. The writing relaxes me. They are entertainments.

I have made a living as an actor for over fifty-seven years. I have a Masters degree in English Literature from Loyola Marymount, Los Angeles; a Bachelor's degree in liberal arts from the University of Wisconsin; and two honorary PHD's, one from Emerson College in Boston, and another from Carthage College in Kenosha, Wisconsin, citing my achievements in the Humanities and the Performing Arts.

Trying to publish is a brand new endeavor. Following the guidelines has been amusing, sometimes perplexing. My life as an actor has been a life of rejection with occasional acceptances, just enough to constitute a minor but substantial career. I have no fear. From here to the end, it's all fun.

My count is bound to be inaccurate. But I get approximately 7000 words in approximately sixty-eight of my computer-printed pages. Should these stories be printed in a book, the total page number will be different.

The "subjects" of the stories vary widely from one another. They are fantasies that explore complex humans in their complex emotional entanglements and physical situations.

Each story takes place in a matter of hours, in one day.

As Edgar Allen Poe advises in his astute literary criticism, a short story should be a compact tale told briefly and intensely, and convey one aura, make one solid impression that resonates during and following its reading. I subscribe to those criteria. Or, to be more honest, that's how these stories turned out. My conscious mind did not set out with Mr. Poe's guide lines. My subconscious ruled. And afterward, I realized what I had done . . . . or tried to do.

The quality of these stories is a matter of individual determination. Everyone is right in his reaction to a written fiction. The entertainment value is personal, a subjective reaction, surely, sometimes followed by an analysis that results in additional pleasure to the reader, or a re-evaluation that reduces his approval.

The stories don't mind.

I am pleased to have them published.

Sincerely,   DANIEL J. TRAVANTI
       Actor

Brown Day

That flash again: "Howaboutacigarette?" I stopped smoking six, no, wait, well . . . . it was last Tuesday night and this is Wednesday morning, so . . . Stop counting! she thought. That floating question-order was a smoky tape unreeling past her from out of a fog bank, barely visible but badgering. It was a turn-on, of course, just like the sex with him. She didn't want it now, today. Anymore. She said she could see herself and Ben, but she could not see Ben alone. It was an old reel. "Howaboutacigarette" Oh, fuck off!

She wondered how that could be. Her film had no sound. She guessed that it was just that certain sensual impressions lingered longer. And are they languorous and loving? Not likely. Yes. Shit, of course they are! But not lately, that's all. Her mind danced one of its word jigs, a favorite pastime to lighten her spirits whenever she felt close to despair. She had lingered too much in the past lately, and she had wondered if she would ever make it to now. Or would it always be just another time to deny. I'm so glad of everything's being then! she thought. It was a motherfucking dilemma. Cole Porter: "It's da limit." Naturally, tomorrow would be better. But I want to be here today! Sonofabitch, a clue. Howaboutacig . . .? Fighting off the temptation, she reeled backwards and slipped again.

She reminisced with a grudge. Mmm, my God, I love you! No! If I can get to like now, I won't have to keep erasing, and tomorrow will be great. Christ, help me!

She put on the copper kettle. It had one of those shapes that make it hard to see the exact middle of the bottom, so she kept setting it down off center of the burner. Drives me crazy! Looks different from every angle. Sometimes the flames would lick up the fat sides and she would watch to see if they would reach the wooden handle. She would have hated to see it happen, but she was titillated each time. The fire played itself and she watched. Copper is golden; silence may be brass. I'm a pot voyeur. Jig. Howabouta . . . ? Kiss. Tongue. Mmmm. Kiss. The pot began to wobble and the loose lid tinkled annoyingly. She centered the damned thing and reached for the phone in the same swoop.

"God, that was fast! It didn't even ring."

"It did. That funny warning-gurgle that the phone company can't explain to me." Off balance, she wanted to scream: at the pot, at the phone, and most of all at him. Goddamit! It was too friendly, too simple. Mmm, cheeks. Mouths. Shit!

"Listen, you're probably pissed off and busy and all that, but I thought I'd take the chance . . . well, I'm glad I got you. It's really good to hear your voice. I mean, it really is. Phew, I've missed you, you know. Fuck! I wasn't going to say that. Big deal. I knew I'd have to. How are you, Heart?"

His casual air and flip warmth curved my spine. I cupped the mouthpiece of the phone with my right hand, the way I used to hold his jaw sometimes, and I hugged the earpiece with my left shoulder, shrugging it hard to my head. My left hand was sandwiched between my thighs.

I was sitting by now but up on my toes, hammering the air with my heels. The Thinker.

Mechanized. I was about to hyperventilate, but I refused. Sweet Christ, I was always refusing.

Only that, nothing else, forever just refusing. That's death!

The kettle tittered. I saw a long, thin black smudge feathered beneath the flame that was slobbering up the side of the pot. It reached almost to the lid, which was askew and lisping. Thppt, shpt, tuppa tuppa tup. Then it spat. I raspberries back at it and Ben was startled. "Oh, sorry," I said, and thought: Thanks, God. And I smiled for the first time that day.

I thought I was relaxed, but I almost fell off the stool. It was an English pub stool, shiny and worn and wobbly with one short leg. Or were three too long? Jig. Thinker athwart. My right shoulder cushioned against the cool brown wall and I stayed there tilted, heels raised but still, thighs unclasped, cheek and left shoulder unclenched, and heart ready. "I'm Okay, Ben . . . I think. How 'bout you?"

"Good, I'm good. I'm really all right. Couldn't be better, you know that?" Jesus, he's always on! Oh, God, no . . . no more. Stop it! He's not always on. He's nervous now. Please keep me, God.

"Don't get mad, but are you calling for a reason? I mean, for more than just to talk? Which is okay, it's enough, and I don't mean to be provocative or anything . . ." I couldn't refuse any longer to gasp, I was about to pass out.

"I know, Heart." He called his son that, and his daughter. They all called each other that in his family. I had loved it, was sent by it, the first time he had said it to me. "I miss you sometimes, that's all." Silence.

The copper was blackened now with a hand-sized splotch. The kettle had skittered off center again. The tam-like lid was cocked and stuck dumb. The water had boiled down far enough to stop splattering out, but there was a pale rope of aged steam wobbling out of the spout. Unsteady and frayed, it rose and fell, curled and rose again, dropping blobs that formed iridescent green pockmarks all over the large black splotch. I leaned over and turned off the flame. My gimpy stool tottered me back to the cool wall, and I heard my breath. Help me, please, I don't want to cry! But oh my, I do.

"What?" he asked, laughing lightly. "What'd you say?"

"Huh? nothing. Oh, hell, Ben, I'm glad you called. I've tried not to need you, and I don't, really. It's just that it's so damned hard to imagine anyone else liking me enough to be with me, you know, during the dull times and loving me anyway, and . . . oh boy, fuck! Thinking about getting to know someone all over again, the idea of starting all over again, well . . . forget it. What the HELL was all that I just said?" I knew he was smiling.

"I love you."

"Anngh. Jeez! Ha, ha, ha. Who did this just now? Did you start it, or did I ?" He did. No, I got carried away. Tears. No. Howabouta . . . ? Peace. Of mind. Peace of heart. Heartfelt. Hearthurt. Heart of whose heart? Hardly hardhearted, but hard to hold. Keep dancing. Help me!

"I guess it's my fault." There was another long pause and I realized I was standing. I don't know when I got up or why, but I felt uprooted and stuck deep at the same time, reeling a bit but glad to be whole and tall. Why was I glad to be tall? Because he wasn't? He wasn't short.

"Are you still there?"

"I'm not always sure." I wondered if he was truly there. As long as two people thrill each other, are in love and within reach, it seems so crazy, such a waste to let anything stop them from being together. Is that it? Is the thrill all that matters? Sometimes. That's petty. But I couldn't feel the thrill unless I loved, could I? Bull. What is love anyway? Stop thinking. "I think I'm your best friend."

"I think you were."

"Oho, past tense?"

"Very tense."

"Careful."

"Always."

I'm hopeless. Go away. Go to . . . Bulgaria, or someplace. Get thee to a coven. But don't die. Oh, God, don't die yet. Kill me first, or at least kill this hurt. I'm an ass. Haha. Oh, no, no, no, no, not too jokey. That wrings the wound.

"Did you deliberately buy me a wobbly stool? It is cute and I love it, but it keeps me off balance."

"I like you that way. I don't mean that in a bad way, really not. Don't get mad now. Oh hell, you understand, I know you do. You're a darling. Oops, I'm making love to you, aren't I? <u>Now</u> you're mad."

"How much have you had to drink, or are you high?"

"One drink . . . you couldn't really tell. That was a guess."

"Well, sort of. I'm presumptuous, I know And suspicious, of course."

"I miss that place on your neck." Oh, no! Kissing me with words. Great at that, the sonofabitch!"

"Jacqueline Susann died today."

"What?"

"Cancer. Fifty-three."

"You're bad."

"I am not."

"You don't hate me. You press your cheek to mine. You kiss your shoulder pretending it's me. You want my leg between yours. You're my lover."

"You're a prick. And don't make a bad joke."

"I kiss you on the mouth."

"Careful, you don't know where it's been lately."

"If you kissed it, it was purified."

It should have been drivel. It was. But not when he said it. Heartheld. I couldn't hear him anymore without smelling him, too. There was a musk, not of cigarettes (Howabouta . . . ?) nor of booze nor breath. Of skin, maybe, or just him. I put my hand on the brown-foiled wall, tan on brown, leaning loving. I knew where I was, but I was lost. I could see out the window. The beige lace half-curtains aged the view and mellowed the already mawkish morning. There was a soft ice-blue sky, filtered and far. The sun seemed pursed, dribbling a dim sheen. The air came moving cool through the splayed louvres, and I felt heady.

"Okay?" "What?"

"Are you okay now?"

"There wasn't anything wrong. What do you mean? I was thinking."

"I know, I heard you. Loud thoughts."

"You piss me off!"

"I know, but I'm cute . . . . for an old fart."

"I'm sorry I hurt you . . . . said all those rotten things. Shit! I feel so fucking guilty all the time. And you know something? Your forgiveness wouldn't make it any easier. I know that, so what's the use?"

"We could forgive each other. Do you think? Could that help? Or would you wonder if I really meant it? I guess. I guess I'd doubt you, too. What does it matter? We could try to be here, now. All right?"

"Sure . . . <u>you</u> do that."

"What?"

"That, all that you said before that I do. Legs and cheeks and . . . you know."

"How did you know?"

"Big deal."

"We really know each other. That's something."

"Hitler and Eva Braun probably knew each other, too."

"Touche! . . . but maybe it's something worth holding on to. Do you think?"

No, goddammit! That's exactly what's most wrong. I don't know yet how to let go, how to be without. I was furious. Did I give him that power over me, or did he always have it? Was that what drew me to him in the first place? "Hey, do me a favor, will you . . . fuck off?"

"Ha, ha, I can't, sweetheart, I'm in no condition. Have you forgotten? Wasn't that one of your foremost complaints at the end there? Easy, now, I'm not trying to make trouble." "Okay, okay, keep laughing till the pain stops . . . even if it kills you."

"Huh?"

"Forget it."

I went away again. There was petulance in my eyes, I felt. Then I saw the anger as I tilted past the little yellow mirror. Was I seeing fury? Why did I feel it first in my eyes? Looking good was part of it, I'm sure. And not seeing clearly into me and us and it all, had to be in the meaning. I was philosophizing again, at a time like that! But I wasn't getting off the line.

Tilted, wobbling, stuttering, gasping, leaning, but standing pat. Thinker writhing.

"I'm going away soon. Did you know?"

"Are you kidding? How could I know that?"

I was still angry, and gave myself away.

"Oh, wait a minute. Sorry. Yeah, well sure, I could've heard it from Mick, but . . . no, actually I've only talked to him twice in, hell . . . oh, God . . . at least three months, it's been.

Pssh. No! Where? This time?"

"Easy. You're so exasperated. Easy, hon. I'll hang up, if you want me to, you know. I mean, I'm glad you've stayed on this long. So I thought you wanted to, at least it was okay to talk. Is it still? Or, I'll stop right now."

"No. I mean, yes, it's all right. I mean, you can't stop now. Yes, sure, I do want to know."

"Spain."

"Oh, great. On a picture?"

"No, just to do it."

"Alone? Forget it. I'm not fishing."

"No, that's all right. I know. With Kitty and Hal."

"Jesus, I'dve thought they'dve been by now."

"They were, have . . . . once before, but only for a week. They're over there waiting for me now."

"Well, Spain sounds a little better than Bulgaria. And in a coven, who knows?"

"You just lost me. Bulgaria? A convent?"

"No, even worse. I'm being bad now. May I just forget it, please?" Nothing. "Okay, I'll tell.

I said a coven. You know . . . a witch's coven."

I'd called him a wizard before, but playfully, with love. I meant to jab, this time.

"Oh, Heart, don't be mean. Please?" Bless the bas-ass. Bless me. Us all. I could smell him again, suddenly. That essence was us, not him!

"Forget it. This is a ridiculous conversation. Wait a minute, I have to think. It's all too fast. Oh, yeah, right. Condition. <u>What</u> condition? What <u>is</u> that?!"

"In a second. It's not important, really, but just wait a minute and I'll tell you. First I want to talk about covens, if you won't get furious."

"Oh, hell, that was practically a compliment. I mean, it was <u>meant</u> as a crack, but you do have that talent, I mean, power, uh . . .shit, I can't even hate you properly!"

"You're the witch. That's what you were calling me, right?"

"Well, yeah. People listen to you, and you seem so together. Mr. Straight."

"No comment."

"I'm glad."

"But, oh, my God, I do talk a lot . . . still. Some of those parties! Flapping my gums from the minute I walk in until I leave. People must think I'm getting senile."

"If they do, they've been thinking that since before you were fifty, and that would make it a weird notion."

"I am weird."

"True. No, come on, you know they love it."

"Well, I guess I'm hopeless. Why do I do it, Heart?"

There he was again, the penitent child. His humility always flattered me. So who was really at fault?

"You never learn, remember?"

He used to say that about himself. It made him seem vulnerable, and it was ingratiating as hell. It excused insensitivity that could drive you to tears. It also tested his credit. Love me anyway, it said. And, see how dumb I can be and still be loved? See how much she cares? It never occurred to him to change. That would have made him responsible, and then the relationship would have been unnecessary. And I knew that all along, God help me! "I know, but I think I'm beginning to."

"Hmmm?"

"Learn."

"Oh, yeah."

"How long has it been since we saw each other?"

"You mean, since we were together? Or since you've seen me? Because I've seen you twice in the last three months. Driving by the apartment one morning, and one time you were up ahead of me on the freeway."

"Aha! Were you glad or mad or sad?"

One of his cute patter questions, the charming sonofabitch."

"Well, oh hell, forget it. It's been about four months, actually. Yes?"

"I guess you're right. Is that the longest . . . ever?"

"Sure, by far. I used to think that would be impossible."

"Me, too. It was."

I poured a cup of water. It was tepid. I reached for the instant coffee. It had a dark taste, but not of coffee. I put in two saccharin tablets, but it wasn't sweet.

"God, enough already! Whatcondition?!"

"You're still relentless."

"And you're provocative still, so drop it."

"I've quit the cigarettes. Sixty-seven days today."

"Really? Great! How do you feel?"

"Fine, now. It was a bitch for the first month, about."

"Oh, I know. I've got eight days. No, seven . . . shit, here I go again! Eight, yes, eight."

"That's shocking. I mean, boy, if you can get off 'em so young, that's terrific. God bless."

"Oh, God bless, from you?"

"He's my god, too."

"Okay. Now tell me, or I'll hang up."

"Condition, right."

The cool brown bore a warm fading handprint. I don't know when I released the wall. The hammering had stopped, my temples were still, the skittering lid was silent, and I was smiling for the second time that day.

"God, I'm tired all of a sudden!"

"Me, too. I'm in the hospital. They're letting me go today."

"Oh, my god, what?"

"I'm all right."

"Sure?"

"I'm sure. You know the thing I've been having in my leg?"

"Yes, I remember, right. Okay now?"

"Well, better. Part of the trouble was the cigarettes, of course. That I knew, and you even said."

"Yeah, right."

"So . . I'm getting better."

"That's it, that's all?"

"Oh, hell . . . no. No, I wouldn't need hospitalization just for that."

"So tell me, goddamit!"

"There was a whole circulation stoppage. They've opened it all up, and I feel a helluva lot better."

"You said that already. I believe you."

"So, that's it. And as soon as the doctor says, I'll be on the plane."

"Have fun."

"Sure. I'm glad I called."

"Me, too."

"It's been hard."

"For me, too."

"Right."

"Be well . . . and happy."

"You."

"Days and days. Time."

"I know. Good trip."

"Thanks. Bye, Heart."

I hung up and slipped back down onto Gimpy, and tottered against the wall. I saw Ben at the ticket counter. I smelled his luggage and felt his nervousness. I rode the escalator with him, and I hugged him away. I didn't stay for the takeoff. I watched the plane come in at Madrid, saw him trip down the gangway, smiling and waving. Kitty was bouncing on Hal's arm, and fluttering back. I began to sweat with Ben. I squinted through the sepia haze with him.

The coffee was bitter all of a sudden.

As Ben pressed down the receiver, the surgeon entered. Ben started, then rolled his back to the doctor as the doctor spoke.

"How are you feeling?"

"Lousy."

"It'll get better."

"Ha! It has to."

"Ready to try the leg?"

"Do I have to?"

"Only if you want to walk."

"To where?"

"Out of here, at least."

"That would be nice. Okay."

"This is Dr. Holvey. And Sylvia."

"Hi."

"A pleasure. I always watch your show. You're terrific."

"Thanks."

"Dr. Holvey will be your therapist, for at least a month, I'm guessing. Wanna sit up now?" It was a struggle, but the titanium limb fit snugly to Ben's left thigh as they helped him try his first step.

Nat said he had an accent he couldn't identify. He was in Del Mar. His name was Miles. He had fixed Nat's bike and charged him very little. Nat was thrifty. I was broke. I started from my house near the beach, taking a chance that the chain wouldn't snap before I found Miles. "Miles-will-fix-it-Miles-will-fix-it," it told me. The sky was clear, but the fog was rolling in. I looked back. I was in the sun, past Lincoln Boulevard. The fog was thick behind me. My face was warm. My back felt the chill of the fog. The fog looked solid, a wall, right at Lincoln.

That's what it did. It rolled to Lincoln and stopped. Something held it back. Temperature? Inversion? You could count on it. You couldn't see the fog when you were in it, only after. You came out, didn't notice, looked back, and there!

I pedaled faster. The chain was silent. Animal hospital on my left. I crossed over the road and rode up on the sidewalk. I didn't remember it this far east. I had taken Kitty there once. They were nice, but I worried. The cages made me sad. The animals talked. Some cried. The attendants knew the difference, didn't they? Faster. Maybe I missed the street.

Nat had given me an address. Five numbers, but he couldn't remember the sequence.

Miles would fix my chain. The chain said so: Miles-will-fix-it, Miles-will-fix-it, Miles-will-fix-it. I should have asked again, but I kept thinking that the numbers would come to me, in the right order. I remembered a seven and a three. I rode up and down streets. All the houses had five numbers. None had a three and a five. Then I recalled that Miles worked in his garage. In an alley! Up and down alleys now, up and down, back, down and up. Frustrating, but exhilarating, too. It was sunny when I started the pattern. I'd gone back west, and it was foggy. Nowhere near Lincoln Boulevard. The fog had made it! Kept rolling in. Slipped through. I felt a chill all around me. Backyards were blurry. Through the mist I heard clanking.

Clank, ping, clink, clang!

It stopped. I waited. Whirring. A bicycle wheel materializing twenty feet away. Wait, wait. A loud plunk. A muttered growl. Silence. I waited. Whirring again. I walked the bike down the alley. It was cobblestone on the sides, black gravel in the middle. Not the powdery kind. Thicker. Neat. Crunchy. I liked the sound of the tires on it. I wanted to feel the cobbles. I walked over them. I expected bumps, but no. Smooth. I liked it.

"You lookin' for help, young man . . . or trouble?"

The voice was deep. The accent wasn't any American I knew. The fog was thicker than I'd ever seen. I couldn't see much past my bike and one garage. The voice glowed in my ears. A wide beam washed over me through the fog. The garage just there was lit like a stage. Curtain up. Or door. Silence. The voice boomed, not first hand, but like an echo. I looked in its direction, into the light. Three shiny bikes stood along a wall. A workbench ran the full length of the wall opposite. Two bikes hung from a beam at the rear. I saw nothing in between at first.

Two steps in, a man materialized. Then a work table, thick, on thicker legs.

"You lookin' for help, young man, or trouble?" Echo, echo, echo. Not sure, but he didn't sound threatening.

"I'm looking for help. My bike is."

A bike was laid out like a puzzle on a blue tarp. The man was bent over a silver frame, held in the vise of a large steel contraption with a heavy base. He was facing me, but didn't look up. "Come in. Come."

He was cleaning the frame. His fingers were short and thick, with white hairs on the knuckles, on wide palms. The nails were manicured. Shiny, but not from grease. His forearms were strong, heavily veined, nearly hairless. His head looked like a white helmet held up by large protruding ears. His glasses were extra-thick. He looked up at me. He was smiling, but his eyes made him spooky. The glasses were so thick that his eyes appeared alternately as black slits for a second, then enormous globes when his head moved. A lighthouse.

I kicked down the stand and set my bike off to the side. I waited for him to speak again, but he worked silently. His hands remained clean. His body barely moved. I waited. The fog was visible in the alley. I felt stalked. I walked out.

Up the alley to the right, high red and pink bougainvillea bushes rose like a curtain. They climbed up over the garage and draped over a neighboring fence. On the left were red and yellow mounds of lantana and spikey blue Nile lilies. Dwarfs. Not really lilies, I once read.

Scarlet roses clung to the other expanse of the roof.

I walked back in and leaned on the end of the long work bench. The man sat very still on a flimsy looking stool for minutes at a time. Then he would spring at a nut or a bolt or a tool like a spider upon its prey. His back and legs would freeze. Wrench and plier seemed to float as he picked and wielded and coupled and placed back down gently onto the bench each tool. His hands looked as if they were spinning imaginary cloth as small nuts and bolts joined smoothly together. I watched this for about twenty minutes. When he was satisfied, he let out an "Ayeh," gripped both of his knees and swung his head around and looked at me. A helmet with headlights. His eyes grew as large as his big lenses, then shrank, flowing back into his skull.

"What's wrong with your cycle? He pronounced it sickle.

"The chain's funny."

"You mean, it makes you laugh, or it's not right?"

"You're a funny guy."

"There you go again."

"Again?"

"I mean, you're humorous . . . you make me laugh. I smiled when I first caught you out of the corner of me eye, which you didn't notice, heh, heh, because I didn't mean for ya to. Interesting word, humor innit? Are you a little bit medieval? An old soul, methinks. You are sanguine by nature, though a little worried at the moment. Eh? Am I right? I am, too."

"Sanguine or worried, too?"

"Hee, hee! Hardly worried anymore. I get bilious people. Don't take them on.

Phlegmatic's okay. Easy goes it. You say "does it, don't ye?""

"May I ask what your accent is?"

"Which accent?"

"Yours."

The headlights fixed on me. His facial expression hadn't altered until that look. I tried to look away. He stared with full eyes. I think I did not blink. I know I did not want to miss a glimmer. I started to speak. His smile said, "Wait".

"Do you?"

"Depends."

"On what?"

"On where you go. Stay home, you haven't enny. Go somewheres else, ye have."

"I like yours."

"You can understand me. That's all that matters. You reckon?"

"I reckon."

I never took my eyes off his hands, except the one time when he fixed me.

"How can you keep your hands so clean?"

"Precision. . . . . . and protective cream. But swiftness is the key. Get in, get on, get off, clean up. That's all life is. Dust. Dirt. Grime. Waste. Then you clean up and start over. First thing, when you die, they clean you up. Better than before. Then they throw you away. Good idea. You had your time, now give over, get out. Make room."

I had many questions but I couldn't think of a thing to say. He finished work on the bike in the vise, grunted, wiped his hands once each with a clean white cloth and with it gripping the frame, righted it and let out a whistle. The discarded cloth landed near my foot. I picked it up to give my hands a swipe and put it on the workbench. It was purely clean.

I folded it and set it down. He walked over to my bike and hoisted onto the spot just vacated. I thought, "Get in, get on." At first he sat and stared at it. He stood up, walked around, and sat again. He touched the chain lightly. He pedaled it with one hand, then two. Silently, I dared his hands to remain clean.

"This'll cost ye."

"I was afraid of that. But I have to have it. I can't spend too much on gas."

"A half hour. Ten dollars. Or, bucks, you say, right?"

I was afraid to question it, so I just smiled and nodded. He looked at me, searching for a response. I tried to look away but could not. I stood up, thinking I would stroll up the alley. He turned back to work and said, "Stay. Ask your questions."

Suddenly the alley was brightly lit. It could only be a headlight. But no vehicle came by.

"What's going on?"

Miles laughed. "Maybe they followed you. Or me."

A brown and white dog trotted by. I looked to his neck. There was a collar. Good. I looked to Miles. He nodded and jerked a long thumb toward the yard next door.. Two black cats came yowling into the space under the narrow bench, playing. I took them to be mother and kitten. The kitten had a half white face but the same pale blue eyes as the adult. The fog was dense and cool. It was entering the garage, but the outside glare grew brighter. I edged out to look. The fog was ten blocks past its limit, blocking the sun. But it blocked the light sensor, too. The floodlight on the corner of the low garage corner redeemed the day. It was eerie and romantic. Milres was a leprechaun in a misty glade. His remark reached my ears late, an echo.

Did he mean the animals?

"You mean the cats?"

"Cats know things. Black ones are witches's familiars. You know what they are? They follow the witch's prey when the witch is busy. They tell things to the witch. Or wizard." He glanced at me. I swear he winked.

"Are you one?"

"Which, a cat? Or a wizard?"

"Oh, come on! Could you be a cat?"

"Sure, I forgot to tell ye. They change back and forth sometimes. Wizard, cat. Witch for a while, then cat. That way, they can escape out of a tight spot. And then, even a human. Or disappear. Or just relax. Witches get tired, too, ye know. Like people. But witches can't rest. Their lists are too long. Like some people's. But they have to get it all done. Cats know how to loll. You know that word? Lolling around, doing nothing? Lolling is okay. Lollygagging is wasting, though. Is it the same in the U.S. of A.?"

"Sure, I'm old enough, and I read. I know how how to loll. But lolly-gagging is only in books."

"Books are good. Best. For information. For having fun, too. Yer best tool. Yer best toy.

Go ahead, ask."

"Do you read minds, too?"

"Only intentions."

I asked him how long he had lived in his house.

"'Tisn't mine. My daughters. I came five years ago, after my gal died."

He said his mother was born in "CAVAN County, Ireland. Northern Ireland! No, not that one!

North in the <u>Republic</u>.

I smiled. Okay. I get it.

They came to Boston when he was fifteen, his sister, nine. His Ma died last year, Pa the year before. They were told witches stories. His sister was a witch. I smiled. He stared at my mouth and tsk-tsked.

His father was Oliver Wilde. Maybe a distant relation. They and his mother, Rose O'Leary

Wilde, moved to Boston to work as domestics for a Kennedy cousin.

"That must have been fun. Did you live in a mansion??

"Ho! We lived in a basement. Of a mansion."

"Was that nice?"

"Hee! It was cozy. We had a garden. I had my own room. The Kennedys were kind."

"Did you fix bicycles?"

"No, I drove, though. A big Bentley. Smelled new for twenty years. I cleaned it. Didn't need much. Developed my technique. That and cream. A secret, but I'll tell ye. Coconut oil.

It goes right into the skin. Hair, too. You can eat it. Witchcraft. Has protection. Antibodies.

Like mother's milk. Witchy. It makes you look good, even your hair, so good you disappear.

Ya know?"

"You mean, invisible?"

"Hee, hee! No, so healthy you glow, right into the air, into the light; not a blot, like sick folks. Unhealthy folks. Glowing folks blend into the life light. People smile at ye, but right through you. Sometimes."

I asked what happened, how he got to Del Mar, California.

"Nora found me. She married me, we had a daughter. Nora died, and I died some, too.

She was my familiar. She left me. But I found her again. Here. In the fog and the sunshine.

Both!

I laughed. "Are you a mystic?"

"Hee! No. No, but I'm a mystery, ha ha."

He told me that his daughter Sara owned the house. It was a craftsman, built in the nineteen teens. A bungalow with a front porch, wide square pillars, deep steps, an overhanging roof that kept the rain off, and the sun, on blistering days. But the fog always crept in 'like a gray hunchbacked thing.'

I wish Nora coulda seen it. She loved the sunshine. Not much of it in Boston, though the winters were brightly lit by the reflecting snow. Nora was like that. Lit by the snow. Glowing even on gray days. We liked New England. New. We never knew the old England. No love lost there. No rancor, though, not really. I was a boy when The Troubles covered us like soot.

Even in the Republic.

He lifted my bike with one hand and set it down at my feet.

"No charge. Don't speed, and say hello to the cats when you pass the hospital."

"How did you know?"

He shook his head, looked down at his toes, and smiled.

"How much do I owe you?"

"You mean, money?" And he winked. "No money. The thoughts were worth ten times."

"More, to me. Would you mind if I visited you some time?"

"No. Thanks."

"Okay. Good."

"No, I mean, no, don't come. . . . . I may not be here."

"But, I thought . . . . "

"You thought we had a darned good time, your sickle is fixed, the fog is almost lifted, it didn't cost you a cent, and you like me. I like you, too. That's enough for me." "You're not . . . .

"Dying? Sure. But not right now. Don't know how soon. No notice yet, if that's what you mean.

"Tata," waving his large right hand raised high over his head as he seemed to fade through the door into the house.

Postcards

He cried occasionally, usually over music. Especially soaring strains of classical symphonies and almost any guitar music. He cried over himself. The music was a movie score that heightened his self-pity. Sometimes the beat caught him, though, and he would glide an invisible partner across the floor for you, puckering his lips and syncopating a step. You had to stare, he was so curious and interesting then. And he knew you had to look. It wasn't even the beat. He might have been dating himself and liking the company, but Jed wasn't even that companionable. John liked him anyway. That afternoon he had to prove it, because Jed was in trouble with his boss again. Harry Erdman liked the way Jed handled customers, but he was jealous of Jed's popularity. Some people, in fact, came to the shop mostly to see Jed and pass a few entertaining moments, not to buy pencils or stationery. Fortunately, though, the shop was located near the bus station, so many strangers dropped in to get an emergency envelope or a pen, sometimes in desperation. The envelope seekers were almost always annoyed to find they couldn't buy just one but had to take the whole bundle.

Jed knew how to handle them, too.

"I'll bet you're like me," he'd croon, "always meaning to write, but never any paper handy, or no envelopes."

"Right on, then you have to get stamps and find a mailbox. Geez!"

"Listen, why don't you get stamps right now and put 'em on each envelope, so you'll be ready when you want to write something."

"I never thought of doing it ahead of time. Great idea," said Lily.

Jed had given the suggestion before, but this time Harry Erdman was listening and watching. He saw the strawberry blonde tingle at Jed's words. Lily bought the packet of envelopes and tingled some more at Jed's touch when he handed her the change. She waved and pouted and flashed quick glances at him as he moved back and forth behind the counter. Finally she beckoned him out from behind his cover, waving in every direction and darting looks around for the stamp machine. Jed's eyes were dark but smiling. He had those thick black brows and long lashes that some dark Irish types possess, devastatingly attractive, as Tyrone Power's were, and lethal. He knew it, and thought he liked the power. Lily was thrilled. Harry Erdman was frightened. Jed had a pale face, epicene almost, but handsome, and appealing to some women. He looked at himself often, in front of the mirror in the back room, in every storefront window, and even reflected in shiny fenders and bumpers. For a long time, Harry Erdman thought he might be narcissistic, but last year when Jed came to work for him, he knew that he was scared. And Jed frightened even more.

The stamp machine spat out two short ten-centers and a long tongue of five ones. Jed popped off the tens and Lily, giggling, plucked the ones. Jed put his arm around her waist and bent his head close to hers. Their backs were to Harry and now their voices were muffled. They weren't entirely still, but sort of jerking as they rubbed against each other and bobbed their heads, first toward the stamp machine, then past each other's faces, Lily's curly hairdo disappearing past Jed's shoulder at first only for a moment, then repeatedly for seconds at a time. Jed's grip got tighter. Harry saw that Jed's hand was lower now, pressing against Lily's haunch. In another second Jed was behind her, hunched over the tiny girl, his head buried past her fluffed curls. The perking changed to a sway, then it stopped, and only Jed's back was visible. They were whispering, and Harry Erdman strained to hear, but all he could pick up were chirps and giggles and breathing.

"Time out!" Harry, startled, straightened up, wiped the perspiration from his upper lip with the little finger of his right hand, scratched the graying hair above his right ear with the same finger, thrust out his chin as he stretched his short neck down and outward, pulling back his jowels in three nervous jerks, and started to shout to the lovers to stop. But his throat was so constricted and his temples throbbed so, that he couldn't gauge his volume or control his tongue. His lips had disappeared, his mouth was stretched open only a slit's width, and his eyes which protruded unnaturally under normal conditions, bulged and swam in black waters now. He looked like a startled frog about to lead for cover. When the cry escaped, it dribbled and squeaked, barely audible except to Zeke (not even to Harry's own ears, which were already full of throbbing), who laughed.

"Shh!" whispered Harry. "I mean, . . . dammit, you shouldn't do that!"

"Do what?" giggled Zeke.

"You know damn well. Sneak up on a person like that."

"I didn't sneak. I always come in this way, and you're almost always standing here spying."

"What?" I am NOT SPYING, and I DON'T SPY! I AM NOT A SPY!!" Harry Erdman was screaming. Terrified and confused and embarrassed, he could hardly contain himself. His stomach was churning, his temples were throbbing louder still, his heart was racing and thumping, but the screams were only oozing out from between his clamped lips. Zeke stifled his own dribbled laughter, catching it in a massive hand and stuffing it back into his large mouth. The excitement ringing in his ears tickled the inside of his head.

Zeke Erdman was the baby of the family, but the biggest person by far. Six-foot three, with a size fourteen foot, a thick square torso stuck with too-short arms pinned at their ends with too-big hands, he looked like one of those disproportioned cardboard placard people drawn by children, misshapen and cut out too sharply at the chin and fingers and nose, a misshapen giant's son out of a sepia fairytale picture book. His head was too small, and his mouth and eyes were too big, and his hair was so thick that it hid his tiny ears and almost covered his bulging, boiling eyes. They went round and round all the time, but not grotesquely, more like a kalei-

27

doscope, within a tight circle, and in a colorful pattern, swimming with joy.

"Oh, Bubber, doncha get steamed. Doncha hate me. Cantcha laugh? Let's see whatcha watchin' Oh, oh, oh, boyoboy! He's doing it again, huh, right there in front of the window and he's knowin' yer watchin'. Mmm, slider over wouldga? Lemme see. That Jedder sure knows how to get 'em to play. They come in here jus' ta get a envelope er stamps an' they get Jeddered. I wish I could . . . ooh, no . . . Ha! That makes me nervous. But I'd like ta try."

"Disgusting, Zeke, it's disgusting, that's all."

"No, I think it's pretty. Feels good, too, I know."

"How do you know that? You just said you never did it. Did you? DID YOU EVER? Harry's mouth literally drooled from the pressure of his clamped lips as the intended shout slithered out.

"No, I jus' know an' I'm gonna do it an' feel good and everything. I'm sorry, Bubber.

Bubber, don't be mad, okay?"

"I'm TRYING TO BE CALM now, brother dear! Hear that? I'm your brother, not your bubber! Hear that? So call me BROTHER!"

Zeke never could say it right, but no one had ever ridiculed him for it. He'd seen Harry mad before, but never this abusive, and the shock of the hurtful tone sobered him. His excited hulk, shoulders hunched, arms taut and fists clenched, straining up onto the balls of his feet so that he'd been looming over Harry's frog figure and casting a giant shadow over the counter just past them into the store, sagged and lost its size.

The shadow crept behind the showcase and the carcass curled in on itself.

"I better get out of here an' get John."

He lumbered through the alley, raising a low gray dust storm that followed his feet like a halo as he scuffled toward John's back door.

"Sit, Zeke, and just breathe. Don't say anything yet. Keep breathing. All right, now? Whenever you're ready, calmly, slowly. Coffee? Here."

"Uh huh. It's a little number that Donizetti added to the opera, a song he had from another time, that he dug out of a trunk or somewhere and threw into a dead spot in the story."

"Opera? You mean, like Jed plays in his room?"

"Sure, and what I have on a lot at the shop."

"Yeah, I thought so. I know. I know. Yeah, and that's just the kinda stuff Harry don't like . . . ."

They were standing just inside, next to the stacks of stationery boxes. The top of the dutch door that separated the storage room from the front was almost completely closed, but a little light shone past the brass latch through the opening, etching a bright triangle that almost perfectly framed the fat little white portable radio teetering on the shelf next to the door.

"Oooh, it's almost falling off," cooed Zeke as he cradled the radio back safely onto the shelf. "Oh, the cord is stuck, an' just about got pulled out of the socket. Oh, Ohboyo! Oh, gawd! Oh,oh!" Zeke had frozen stiff, his hands still on the radio, his body blocking the light and throwing a huge folded shadow across half the room and upon the ceiling.

John looked behind the stacked boxes and at first saw only a foot, Harry's thicksoled loafer hanging half off it and wedged between his toes and the wall. Even John, who was unusually calm in tense situations, closed his eyes momentarily before he was willing to look for more. Zeke was still a statue. As he unsquinted, John saw a second shoe, a wingtip, securely on, bent at the toe, facing the dangling loafer, like a penitent kneeling in a confessional. Only this much shone clearly in the triangle of sunlight. The rest was in shadow and obscured, on top of that, by the tension in John's eyes and by the blur caused by their adjustment from the brightness of the alley to the gray stockroom. They were in an embrace!

"Don't look, Zeke."

"I can't even see . . . . what? What?! Oh, oh. . . . Jed!"

As John's eye traveled up the back of the first kneeling figure, he knew Jed's back and searched it for the wound or the tear or some blood. But he saw only Harry's arms resting limply across Jed's shoulders, the left had barely holding the little finger of his right, pressed between the fingers of

Harry's right hand a crumpled piece of paper, no, a snapshot, no, a . . . . yes, a photograph. Without moving, Jed spoke. "Come on in and join the fun, whoever you are."

"My God," thought John, "he doesn't even know who it is, and doesn't care." The music on the radio stopped and the announcer's voice told them about the folk dance recital coming to The Freedom Hall auditorium. Dancers from the "far corners" of Soviet Georgia had been gathered together and shaped into a "precision unit" that nonetheless "retained the exuberance, color and childlike fun" that are still celebrated characteristics of the Georgian peoples. "Come and share the fun," wooed the announcer, "while enriching your cultural experience."

Jed was untangling himself from Harry's still limp figure, leaving Harry a downcast bundle in the chair. Zeke was whimpering against the door jamb, hugging the radio as if it were a friend, and John was giving Jed a hand to get to his feet. Harry's right hand still held the snapshot, turned at last outward so that John could make out three figures on a porch, but no details of their faces.

A half hour later, in John's shop, the glow from his fireplace illuminated the photograph, giving it a soft sepia tone, but at last John could see clearly Harry, about age eight, standing on the top step holding the porch column with his right hand, his left on Jed's shoulder as Jed sat at his feet, while on Jed's lap sprawled a large-headed baby with strangely pendulous arms. Zeke stood stretched across the rolltop, eyes watery and calm, at last, waiting for someone to answer the questions hopping in his head. John handed the photograph to Jed, but he waved it toward Zeke. Zeke held the snapshot close to his nose, more as if he were smelling than looking at it. And indeed, he wasn't seeing it at all.

When Jed finished his confession, Zeke wanted to hug him and hit him and bite him and kiss him. His fists pounded his temples as if trying to throttle the jumble into order. Harry was staring at his blurred image in the fireplace fender while Jed slowly traced short lines of dance steps back and forth between his brothers.

"You have to forgive me, Jed, you just have to."

"For what, old boy?"

"For not telling you I knew, for spying on you, for blaming you."

"No problem, cha, cha, cha. When did you know?"

"When you came for the job. But I didn't want to hope too much."

"Didn't you hate us?"

"NO, Jed, no, no, no. I was scared. I wanted it to be you, but I was scared. I was scared of you when you were little, did you know that? You were happy. You danced. I liked it, but It scared me. It scares me now. I just wished I could.

"Did you recognize me?"

"No. I mean, yes, I mean . . . I wasn't sure about the face, but you have a way of stepping, you know, and when you danced around, phew, it gave me goose bumps! Like then. I never could get it, you know, like, WHY you would just go away, no note or anything. And no postcards. I always looked for postcards. I would read any other person's card and pretend it came from you, no matter what it said. Because it might be from you. I mean, it COULD, you know?"

"Mama wouldn't let me."

"What?"

"Mama wouldn't let me write."

"Didn't Mama love us?"

"I think so. I don't know."

"Did she hate Pop and me, and Zeke?"

"No. But she never loved Papa. She told me in the hospital that that was her sin, and God gave her Zeke as a punishment. Her fault.

Jed danced the quick short toe steps just to Harry's knees, then stood there cupping Harry's face in his large hands.

Harry stared at the floor. "I have been so afraid that it would happen to me. Every day. Looking at myself all the time, waiting for my eyes to bulge. Oh, God, whenever I was a little puffy some mornings, I would just shake!"

"Harry, poor dear Harry. It's not going to happen now. Anymore, dear brother. Mama was afraid. She thought it was her fault. The doctor said it wasn't. She said the doctor didn't understand. Mama loved Zeke, but she couldn't look at him. She said when he hugged her, she felt ashamed."

"She told you that?"

"Only last year, when she was sick. Before she died she said for me to go back. "

"Didn't you ever ask her why she left us?"

"She said I wouldn't understand, I was too little. Then I forgot. She brought it up again when she got sick."

And then when you came right in here every day, and talking to me and carrying on like you do. Every day. And not knowing. Not telling me. Oh! It's my fault. I should've talked about it."

"When did you know ?"

"For sure? Yesterday."

And they explained to each other. But the explanations were not their truth. Zeke knew best. That Harry and Jed had known and loved each other once, that they loved each other still but didn't know each other now, that Harry and Jed loved him and Papa. In his kaleidoscope, they twirled together round and round like the Georgia dancers. Smiling.

Jed had been terrified of Zeke's affliction, as frightened as Harry. Harry thought Jed didn't care. Dancing through jobs and women and single rooms, syncopating fear away, while Harry trembled every day and tore at his dim memory of Jed, clawed at his images of Jed having a good time and sleeping peacefully without the dread that Harry bore. A ghostly figure, vague. The little boy he barely remembered. He felt that Jed had escaped the fear. But Harry was trapped. Jed had all the girls and all the good times.

"But I can't have any, brother dear. I heard the doctor, but I can't chance it, you know? Getting it or passing it on. Can't even dance in one place too long. Not even here. Attachments happen. Didn't have to remember to address postcards, because I wasn't sending any."

Two days later they all went to The Freedom Hall to see the Georgian dancers. Lily liked everything best. Zeke preferred the acrobatic country-comic skits, Harry saw almost nothing, and John and Jed paid half attention, sharing their experiences between numbers, stuttering to catch up.

"I'm afraid, Jed."

"Of what?"

"That you'll go away again."

"I have to."

"Why? Don't you want us anymore?"

"I do, but I have business."

"Oh, sure. Stuff to do."

Jed smiled. "Yeah, a bunch of stuff to clear up."

"Are you in any trouble? Can I help?"

"You already do."

Lily begged for the job and Harry gave it to her. He thought his spying days were over, but as more and more young men seemed to need Lily's help finding just the right birthday or Mother's Day card, the vicarious pleasure soothed his nerves. Zeke was grateful. John was relieved.

Zeke stayed with John more and more. He slept in the small cupboard just inside the alley door, where a tiny window showed him the cinders and flowers outside. Lily looked in on him on her breaks. Mostly she would talk nonstop about a movie or the latest squabble at home or Harry's unpredictable moods. Almost every time, she finished by asking about Jed. "He sends me postcards."

"Oh, my, really? Since when?"

"Since the day after he left."

"Where'd it come from?"

"Him."

"I know it came from him, silly, but what place?"

"I don't know. From his heart." Lily just stared.

Zeke kept his postcards in a stationery box under his bed. He read one every day.

Over and over, if he didn't have a new one.

"How is he?"

"He's coming back."

"He is? Oh, my, oh, oh, he says so?"

"No, but he is."

"Oh, Zeke!""What?'

Lily gazed into his eyes and swore she saw the kaleidoscope. Zeke didn't blink.

She smiled and said, "I believe you."

Then she stood very still as she always did, listening to every word as Zeke slowly read the latest message. She smiled and curtsied, a quick shallow dip at first, which deepened over the months, signed with a giggle in the beginning, which sometimes turned tearful and finally faded just as she went out the door.

Switchback

At the first switchback I admired the fallen branches. They looked natural and still alive, not chopped and dead like the fence. I picked a bouquet of dry twigs. Usually I carried it all the way to the top and back and almost always dropped it before I got back to the house. This time I would keep it. I felt guilty not sharing the walk with the dogs. Selfish. I saw that the branches in my hand weren't all dead; a few were fresh. I liked the contrast of the grayish silvery aged saber-shaped eucalyptus leaves with their metallic beige pods next to the bright green round young leaves. The scent was soothing. A sudden warm breeze through the creaking trees made me shiver. Eucalyptus trees keened. The high pitched squeal sounded human. Maybe they were expressing their disappointment. They were originally imported from Australia to supply railroad ties, only no one bothered to test the wood. Turned out it was crumbly, not at all dense enough to support heavy weight. Alive, they twisted in the wind. Many were blown flat all over southern California. But not before littering hillsides and roads , driveways and swimming pools with masses of sere and new leaves. The entrepreneurs forgot to import the koala bears that kept the trees tidy while providing nourishment. Vigorous and unpruned, they grew even faster, which was one of their other attractions to the railroad visionaries. Abandoned as useful timber, thousands provided wind breaks, writhed in rapidly growing numbers along roads and bordering farm yards and housing developments, and cried in the wind.

The sun departed as the path rose. Then it reappeared at the bend, lighting the soft brown mound where the road switched sharply back. Palpable and frivolous, it seemed, a knowing force. I hadn't slept very well, so I thought I must be tired – though I seemed wide awake – because I was worried.

Now and then I could hear a car or a leaf blower. The birds were giddy, which seemed odd on so still a day. Then all hell broke loose. A bluejay began to squawk. It sounded like an irate boss or a drill sergeant, not like a bird at all, a bigger presence, more knowing. That was wacky. Then I saw it. Big and bossy, all right, and furious at a pair of doves. Jays were bullies. I'd seen them before harassing smaller birds; even squirrels and cats. When they went after those, I figured it was strictly tyranny. This attack was for food, a practical matter. Or was it gluttony? Can birds overeat? A fat lumbering bird on the ground or straining to glide over hedges without hooking its landing gear suddenly seemed possible and hilarious.

The jay was watching me, I knew it. I looked around and finally spotted him by staring straight ahead for the longest time. It was as if he'd been there all along and suddenly materialized like the Cheshire Cat. His eye was on me, all right, but askance. Birds have to look at you sideways, but I never knew it could feel so calculating, so thoughtful, ominous.

I was worried about the mortgage, always the mortgage. The argument with Luce wasn't unusual or harsh, but hurtful because we were both afraid of the job change, I more afraid than she, actually, but still she had been outraged, really offended, which seemed like a terrible over-reaction, though I didn't say so or even give her a hint that I thought so, so I didn't think I was the cause of her exceptional hurt. But I worried about it.

Suddenly there was screeching and fluttering and chatter and a rush of wind. But it only seemed like actual wind. There were the jay and two very fat birds, so overweight that I had the spooky sensation I had dreamed them up and made them appear, only these weren't at all amusing. They were smaller than the jay, but more threatening, like pudgy gray Sumo wrestlers, a tag team against the bright blue loner. Their thrashing in the branches looked random, even chaotic at first, but as I stared I saw that the two defenders were the antagonists, and the jay was fighting for his life.

I wanted to watch. I wanted to see what happened next, but I needed to walk and enjoy the day. It was too late. Even if I enjoyed the scenery, how could I forget this fight? I had to get away, but I couldn't move. For a few seconds I lost sight of the birds, but the flapping leaves showed me where they were. They were completely hidden but louder than before, invisible screechers clawing or pecking, I couldn't be sure, but battering the air and foliage. Feathers flew, so I knew blows were connecting, then suddenly all was silence.

Some branches bobbed, small twigs fell with some leaves, there was rustling. I was frozen. I thought of blood and realized I was staring hard for it. Drops or streaks or gobs, maybe. Or what? Was I wishing for red specks or torn flesh, verifiable carnage?

How could I want that! Where were they? If I could only see them again, safe; though I knew some damage must already have been done. Maybe I needed to see them again to confirm that I hadn't imagined it all. They were gone.

No! How could they do this to me, upset me like this, promise me blood and guts, a victor, a loser, a dead body? Keep walking. But I sat down on a pile of leaves, covered my face with both hands and checked my breathing. I felt my pulse. It was fast. I had been in that fight. I was beaten and bloody and alone again.

Please come back, I thought, and realized I was saying it out loud. My hands were sweaty and red. I had been squeezing the branches and their imprint was on my palm and fingers. A small blood blister ached beneath my wedding band. I made it to the top. Five minutes later I had forgotten the whole thing. Until a jay flew onto a branch just at the edge of the dirt path on the last curve before the ranch house came into view. I was at the polo field of Will Rogers Historical Park. It stretched for at least a hundred yards, green and cool but cozy in the embrace of the white plank fence on three sides and the enfolding grassy slope on the long opposite length.

A couple was on the knoll playing with their little girl. A young man was flying a kite, stretching like a dancer to will the red dragon to stay up. Its yellow tail swirled and darted and brought down its own head in a suicidal stranglehold, almost to the ground. The kiter's effort to keep it from crashing felt desperate even from so far away. The little girl stared at the kite and raised her arms to help it or maybe to clutch the writhing creature, and called to it. I wondered if she meant to call it down or to inspire the demon to soar. Grasping and calling, she looked about to tumble to the bottom of the slope. Her father laughed and rolled toward her to keep her from falling. I hadn't moved. The jay was still, too.

In that second the horse appeared. It must have been on the field but I hadn't noticed. It headed for the child and the man, but the rider jerked away and continued to gallop, toward the kiter, looking first at the couple he had just missed and then straight at me. The horse was white, mottled from his saddle to his tail with splotches of black and gray. He was lean and tall and seemed sure of himself. The rider was not as confident. Then I saw the mallet, dangling loosely behind his right leg. There were no other riders, so I hadn't thought of polo, and horseback riding was common in the park, so it did not occur to me at first that anything unusual was happening.

Maybe he was practicing. He wore a helmet, and the merest glimmer of a suspicion lit a corner of my mind. It was enough to get me moving. As I strode across the grass I noticed that the mallet was being held now with the tip pointing forward, not broadside as if preparing to hit a ball. Funny, I had thought for years that it was miraculous that players could strike a ball on the run with that tiny tip, until I learned that it was turned the other way. Stupid.

I don't know the first thing about polo matches. I always worried about the horses when I saw teams in the movies. When I was a boy, in the forties, polo matches were in the newsreels in theaters. There was a famous playboy who went around with rich heiresses and pretty starlets. He was a top polo player, rumored to be hung like one of his chargers. A human stud mounted on a stud. The mythical Satyr. But roaming the forests, not galloping and twisting in frenzy to whip a ball into a net.

He looked like a man on a mission. Other people began to notice. He walked his horse at first, but slowly accelerated up one side of the long field, and then spurred to a full gallop across and then up the other long side. Small groups of people rose from their blankets and stared at the handsome rider and beautiful mount. Children shouted and cheered, as if urging him to score a goal. But there was no contest. No ball. No other riders.

The little girl watched the kite and raised her arms to help it or clutch it, against all the odds, it was impossible to tell which, and called to it while her father laughed and rolled toward her to stop her from tumbling down the slope. I didn't move. The jay was still, too.

In the split second that I glanced over at the jay, the horse reappeared in my vision. It came from my right. The rider jerked it away from the child, but directly toward the kite flyer, looking first at the little girl then straight at me. The kiter kept running, at the bottom of the slope, on level ground now, so he must have felt safe with all that green carpet of runway before him.

The horse was gray and black and white, lean and tall and sure of itself. The rider was not as confident. Then I spotted the mallet again, loosely dangling behind his right leg. Since I hadn't noticed a ball or another rider, I hadn't thought of a contest. All I kept thinking was that the mallet was still being held with tip pointed forward.

We were on an historic field. It had belonged to Will Rogers, a legendary satirist, comedian and vaudeville performer in the Ziegfeld Follies on Broadway, movie star, columnist and world traveler. He died in a plane crash while heading across Alaska to Russia. He was going to report back over the radio and in the newspapers how much alike we all were, the Americans like the Eskimos, and the Russians like them and himself and all the rest of us. "I never met a man I didn't like," was his most famous pronouncement. He said it sometimes while twirling a lariat around his feet dispensing droll wisdom over the footlights and the airways. He played polo here. His house on the highest point above the polo field was an historic monument, open for tours. Will had built a tree house on a remote spot of the large property, as a retreat. He had intended to hide out from time to time, he said, from all the attention of all those people he liked. But he did not live to see the tree house again.

Had the polo guy taken the self tour with the portable recording and the earphones? Did the kite flyer take the tour? Most likely, he and his wife did not want to bore their little girl, probably anxious to fly the kite. The chiaroscuro horse kept coming, the rider still looking in my direction.

The scream started just as the little girl tumbled out of her father's grasp toward the kite flyer's feet. It was a high pitched child's distress signal, a rescue cry. The young man's legs were churning as he struggled to keep his balance now, never mind the kite, but the cord was tangled around his arm, apparently, because I could see him scratching at it as he skidded off balance to release it with his free hand. He couldn't avoid the little girl, however, and she whipped like a rag doll flung through the air, at his heels. I was running as hard as I could, not that I thought I could get there in time, but maybe my shouts and energy could somehow turn aside the tumbling body or cause the young man to change direction. I saw the birds in my mind, the splotches of blood and a torn wing. My temples ached, and my right thigh. "No, no, no!" I heard. Then louder, "No, stop, stop, nooo!" I looked toward the young couple, thinking the father was yelling, but in that second the charging horse cut off my view. The voice was mine.

I was close enough to see the kite flyer's eyes and it almost froze me. I was in slow motion, my legs rubbery and sneakers filled with lead. He was not just shouting, his ragged screech was desperate, pleading at the highest human volume, and his eyes were slits dribbling tears, disbelieving the certain disaster. I was maybe twenty-five yards away from the horse and rider, but the scene suddenly grew enormous, as if I were watching from the front row of a theater. Then the reel went fast-forward and stopped so suddenly it took my breath away.

As the little girl hit the young man's feet, her father reached her, snatched her in his arms, rolled over once and held her straight up in safe suspension. The mother was next to them in an instant, sharing the weight and shielding her husband and the child from harm. The kiter was falling in my direction and I saw familiar blood but never such pain. His face was glistening with sweat, his mouth was open and twisted, his forehead a bloody matted sponge. I almost fainted. I couldn't stop my momentum, and we tumbled and rolled first together and then in split directions, as his limp form slipped down the last incline of the hill.

I lay with my face in the grass, my heart hammering the ground, relieved to be still and seeing nothing. But in my mind's eye: horses's hooves, wings, kite, blood, feet, faces, the mallet. The mallet! The rider. I opened my eyes but did not look up. I was sighting down the blades of grass at an angle, facing back toward where I had started. A horse was galloping away, throwing up clumps of turf and gravel. A foot without a shoe stuck up in the foreground. I wanted to be home. I wanted to wish it all away.

My blood thirst had brought this. I had wanted the birds to come back and finish it. I had willed the jay's return but couldn't get him to stay. I got this, instead. Because Luce was right. I was petty. Irresponsible. I had carped about every household decision. I had neglected Tommy, too afraid to talk about the pressures I felt. Over the mortgage. The job I hated. Luce thought she was my problem. And I let her think so. Rotten.

"Luce, I'm not a monster. I ran toward the trouble today. I shouted, got involved. I tried to help. I don't know how to get rid of my fear, that's all. I don't know how to face it. Don't make me get up. This isn't real. It's a dream. The birds weren't real. Shit! I thought I was trying to stop an accident. Or maybe a crime. The whole day is a nightmare."

The nightmare was spreading, in black and white with gray clouds splitting like amoebas , doubling on the horizon, over my head. The shank of a horse, a feathery tail, a bouncing mane, red balloon, red blood. Is the little girl all right? Out of my right eye, just up the slope, I could see the family. The child was crying. Her mother, trembling, was smoothing her hair, daubing her eyes and cheeks, kissing her tiny lips, her neck, her finger tips, whispering between caresses: "It's not your fault, sweetie. No, no, shh. Shh. It's all right. Everything's all right." I felt all of it. I raised my head and located the father. He was on his hands and knees about to reach the kiter, who lay twisted at the bottom of the short slope to my left. "Oh, no. Oh, my God."

I stood up just as the two park rangers skidded to the father, one of them almost trampling me. The other embraced him to prevent a collision, then the three just stared. The young man's temple was pulsating, blood flowing out like water from a bubbler, his face twisted and his mouth distorted, held open at the corner by the weight of his head, which had driven into the soft turf. One of the rangers, a young woman, broke away and scrambled back up the slope. Picnickers and men in shorts, some of whom had been playing soccer at the far end of the field, and hikers and visitors to the historic house gathered close. No one was talking. Another group came running from the stable area along the bottom of the field, shouting.

They wanted to know what happened. Someone yelled, "Did the rider have anything to do with it?"

"I'll bet he did."

"You saw him? Where did he go?"

"I don't know. He just went down the trail. Did you know him?"

"It wasn't one of our horses."

"Is someone hurt?"

Some gasped, when they saw the bloodied kiter, and looked away. Did anyone know him? Is the ambulance coming? Paramedics? Are the police on the way? The siren screeched around the bend of the parking lot and a few people scattered to rejoin friends and children left behind. Others gathered up blankets and baseballs, soccer balls, footballs and picnic baskets. By the time the paramedics got to the boy, the crowd was a mass spreading like a vast puddle, reaching across the width of the field and spilling on to the black macadam, flowing into vans and sports cars and small trucks.

In a small corral a half mile below the field, off the edge of the stream that bordered the State Park, the big tri-colored stallion was sweating. White foam bubbled at the crease of its shoulder and up both sides of its neck. He champed at his bit as the rider slipped it off. His heavy breathing and gasping for air sent spittle flying as he snorted, and repeatedly snapped his giant head down and around, sloughing off the bit and the reins, and shimmying side to side as the saddle was lifted off. He pawed the gravel with all four hooves, and kept shaking off what were now only the lingering impressions riders and tackle leave when a captive mount is free at last. The horse closed its eyes and was suddenly still, understandably fatigued, seeming to doze. Its shimmering damp body shivered in the dappled sun filtering through the trees and the wooden slats of the stable.

Two men suppressing rage ran from their wives that sunny summer day. I stumbled, crying, down the twisting trail back to my house in the canyon, along part of the same route the horseman had to take. I only half-wished I might spot him. On the road at the bottom, a beetle was idling, three teenagers in tank tops and baseball cap and wild hair were looking around. I asked if they had seen a horse and rider. One said he had caught a glimpse back behind him where they had entered the canyon. The others said they had seen no one. An echoing shout rose from the polo field above us. The driver asked if anything was "going on." The girl asked if anything was wrong? I took her to mean based on the grim expression on my face and the still visible wiped- away tears.

"Yeah, something bad, real bad."

The girl said, " Are you all right? Do you need help?'

"Thanks, no. I'm all right, but something terrible happened up there." This over my shoulder as I swung into my driveway.

The man in the stable entered his mansion, poured himself a large tumblerful of scotch, sat down sipping it, breathing hard and wiping his face and neck and arms with a yellow beach towel, then chugalugged the rest, closed his eyes and reached for his cell phone. The sound of sirens was close. He listened and dialed 911 with one thumb and confirmed the address to the dispatcher. A woman's voice from another room trilled, "Hi! You're back early. Everything okay?" No answer. "Are you all right? How was your ride? Everything fine?"

"No."

He unlocked the hidden compartment in his upper right desk drawer and pulled out the polished Glock 23. The pistol had been fired exactly thirteen times, at the gun range in Calabasas, wiped clean, and placed on a blue silk polishing cloth in the hidden drawer. He checked the full new magazine and snapped it in place. He sank down into the large corduroy armchair until his elbows rested symmetrically and flat on its wide arms, facing the front door. His right hand gripped the cool metal the way he'd held the warm Polo mallet. Through clenched teeth he muttered, "Lucky thirteen?"

The police arrived in ten minutes. Two patrol cars and a S.W.A.T. team in a gray Hummer. Six officers all with guns drawn cautiously entered the unlocked front door.

The Green Restaurant

He walked across the street to the bar. A dog came around the corner from the alley. It had three legs. It walked past Brett, stopped to pee on a bicycle and continued on into the restaurant through the door Brett politely held open for him. The sun was bright but the air was cool, inside and out. In the bar, four people sat at a corner table. The dog sat down in the middle of the room at first, rotated his head like a lighthouse beaming, froze when his gaze reached the corner table, trotted to the bearded man and plopped down on his protruding foot. The bartender left a tray with three bottles of beer on it, three glasses, and a shot of whiskey.

Brett seated himself at the end of the curved bar, facing the trio at the table. As the bartender returned to his station behind the bar, wiping it as he settled, without looking directly at him asked Brett, "What can I do for you?" He wasn't thirsty, but he ordered a pina colada and a glass of water.

The woman in the quartet at the table crossed her legs. She wasn't wearing stockings. One of the men laughed and sipped his beer. She took the bottle from his hand and chugalugged most of the contents. One of the other men, the short balding one, stared at her.

At the corner of the bar, Brett downed his pina colada too quickly and ordered a bottle of beer. He could see through the big picture window out to the street. A parade was passing by, but there was no music. The door was ajar, but there was no sound. A drum major was strutting vigorously and conducting, all right, but it looked like a silent movie. He looked at the bartender for an explanation. The bartender shrugged his shoulders and went to the open door to listen. He looked back at Brett and shrugged again.

Brett thought of going back to the hotel, but the paper in the type-writer there bothered him. He took out his notebook and jotted down a sentence. Then another sentence, following the last thought in the previous paragraph in the machine. He drank a toast to the bartender, who smiled at him, and walked out with a beer bottle in his hand.

As he stepped onto the sidewalk, the dog reappeared, on a leash held by a tall fat man with a long white beard on a strangely small cherubic face. Brett raised his bottle, smiled at the man and pointed to the dog, lifting his right leg slightly. When he was out of sight of the bar window, the woman in the bar caught up with him and took his arm, pressing her cheek into his shoulder. A breeze caught her thin skirt and carried it up to reveal her thighs. She pushed it down without looking, or moving from his side. The smile on his face made the corners of his eyes wrinkle. She touched his cheek, pointing to one eye.

"Yeah," he said, and squeezed her closer.

About ten yards from the bar, Jackie's left eyes searched the street for her two previous companions. Brett showed no notice.

"Are they coming?" She shoved a left fist of knuckles into his side.

They weren't coming, but they were following. One street over, in a low black sedan. Short-baldy was driving and looking around. Another man sat slumped in the passenger seat, facing straight ahead. In the back seat a three-legged dog was licking the face of a rigid fat man. The man made no move to stop him. After four blocks or so, he brought out an unusually large red and black checkered bandana and quickly ran it over his face and head, then carefully over his beard, separating the strands patiently until he was satisfied. The dog disappeared from sight as the car turned the corner.

Directly in front of it, Brett and Jackie were crossing the street. The bearded man leaned forward. The driver stared straight ahead. When the car was about twenty feet from the corner, Brett and Jackie stepped off the curb. The sedan accelerated. The couple didn't notice, but increased their pace when a pickup truck turning the corner between the sedan and them sounded a loud squawk on its horn. The sedan blared back The couple stepped back up onto the high curb and turned back to see what was the matter. Jackie kept hold of Brett but tilted to brush away the hair from her left eye. It was damp from being pressed between Brett's shoulder and her forehead. As she flicked her fingers to clear her view, the spike heel of her right pump caught a raised chunk of broken pavement, throwing her off balance.

It seemed that only Jackie heard the gun shot that came from behind the beard in the sedan. Squealing tires and horns masked the sound as Jackie, frightened, and stifling a nearly irrepressible scream, took advantage of her stumble to drag Brett back, steadying them both and twisting them back into the restaurant.

The driver of the pickup truck, stretched half out of her window, screamed : "Fucking hearse!" Short-baldy flipped her the finger.

In the vinyl booth, Brett started giving his order to the waitress.

"Are you all right?"

"Sure, why?"

"I thought I heard something. Then a voice."

"It did look like a hearse."

"No, before that."

"Me, groaning. I cracked my heel." She held up the crimson shoe for inspection.

"I love your shoes." Taking the wounded pump in his hand: "Too flimsy for walking, but sexy as hell. You've got the legs."

"And the nerve."

"I'm losing mine."

"What do you mean?"

"did he say much?"

"What do you mean, you're losing your nerve? You're as relaxed as I've ever seen you." She took his hand and leaned forward. He was still, staring into space over her shoulder. She moved her other hand over his and rubbed the back of it.

"Age." She tilted her head in a way she had, and pursed her ruby lips, revealing a tiny bit of tongue.

"You're tired. Maybe you've just had enough."

"A long time ago."

The chirpy waitress returned with a bowl of vegetarian chili, a basket of warm brown bread and a cup of coffee for Brett, and a Caesar salad with extra dressing on the side for Jackie.

"My slurpie?"

"Ooops, sorree! No problema. It's right back there screaming for me. Back in a jif!"

"What does she mean, no problem?"

"She just talks off the top of her head, that's all. Does he really think bullfighting is a sport? And hunting . . . and stock car racing?"

"Who?"

She poured half a cruet of dressing on top of her salad and mixed it with her fork and Brett's coffee spoon, tasted a large forkful, making sure to stab three slivers of anchovies and a good portion of hard-boiled egg, swallowed and wiped her lips using both hands, careful not to smear her heavy lipstick.

"Raul? Yeah. He spoke few words but told me a lot. And deep sea fishing. He doesn't read, you know. Books, I mean."

"He's the old friend?"

"No, that's Robert, the short sexy balding one."

" Hmm. You never called him sexy before."

"Oh. Didn't I? Well, he is. To some people . . . to Raul, obviously. I mean, oh, shit!"

"Never mind. Does he read?"

"Oh, yeah, a lot. He doesn't look it, but he's bright, very bright."

"What does a bright person look like?"

"Not like him. You look bright, very bright."

"I've made too many mistakes here."

"No, it's going to work out." She ate a big mouthful of salad, took a couple of strawfulls of slurpie, wiped her mouth again, crossed her arms on the table and, staring at his averted face, said, 'Why did you let them see you?'"

"Challenging the Furies. Only these are men."

"They're boys. Big bad boys. Big very bad boys."

"I don't want to hide anymore. I want to get it over with. So I can write."

"What if they kill you?"

"Then I couldn't write anymore."

"Stop it! They're probably following us, you know. In fact, I'm sure of it."

"I think the dog lover took a shot at us. At me."

The piece of bread in her throat made her gag. Her eyes exploded, relaxed, and set their gaze on his chin. In a measured tone she said, "You're not only tired, you're crazy."

"I know, it's too much for me."

"But you're right. I heard it."

"Now do you believe me?"

"So, what do we do?"

"Finish eating and I'll tell you."

"So, when the writing's not happening, you're so bored you can't sit still?"

"No, I read a lot, you know."

"Not enough. You haven't read lately about big bad guys who just like hurting people."

"You believe that? That motives don't count? They just do it for kicks?"

"I do. I'm so bored reading about the difficulty of establishing a motive. And about details of the latest atrocity in Angola and Bosnia. The details are supposed to explain why the enemy did such a horrible thing. Bull! I know why. They liked it. The motive for murder is murder. They've always liked it. They just couldn't get backing, so when half-wits in charge say it's okay to go get them, they're liberated. The law is on their side. The trouble is, when the ruling jerk-offs are dead, the killers can't stop. They don't want to."

"Why are you here?"

She looked at him for a long time, chewed off a corner of whole grain bread, and said, while chewing, "You're a good listener."

"I never heard you talk this much."

"I'm nervous. Scared . . . . spitless, you moron."

"I know, you love me."

"Thanks."

The sedan passed by the restaurant four times while they were inside. Brett saw it twice. Jackie caught it once, reflected in the mirror above the bar behind Brett. She saw it pull up, back up, pull up again, then back into an open spot just barely out of sight. She excused herself and walked toward the restroom, which was in the rear, but she chose the longer route past the window in the front. She glanced back at Brett and entered the restroom. She saw what she had suspected. Two spots behind the black sedan was the pickup truck, with a woman behind the wheel. Taking her seat a few minutes later, she nonchalantly finished her salad.

"What did you see?"

"Oh, you! Who does the pickup truck belong to?"

"Sam."

"Oh, God, why the hell do you do this?"

"I don't cook . . . or shop."

"Your wife drives a pickup truck?"

"Not all the time, but she owns it. The people at the nursery use it mostly, but Samantha picks up stuff from the hardware store and the markets."

"Do you know what it's doing out there now?"

"I guess she's following me."

Jackie kept her eyes off Brett for at least three minutes, wondering what she was going to say next. Brett thought she would be right to explode. He waited for it. He thought the gleam of pale sunlight on her long blonde hair the warmest color he had ever seen. She was a vision, only half visible in the hot glare that blurred her form just below her breasts, like an unfinished master sketch, tinted, still but alive, and impossibly real. She was relishing her food, in a reverie that made him horny. "Are you with me?"

"Hmm?" Her eyes met his and marked the glint of anxiety in them. Her chewing slowed but remained concentrated. Neither looked away, as she wiped the corner of her mouth, made sure her fingertips were clean and put all the silverware was back in place. After a sip of his beer, she folded her arms and continued.

"You shouldn't have walked out with that bottle of beer. You could have been ticketed."

He was smiling slightly, but his eyes were gleaming and wet.

"I'm here," she said.

"But are you with me?"

She would have told you that this year they had spent together was the happiest yet for her. She would have told you that never before had she felt helpless in the company of a man. Not weak, not exploited, but powerless to resist his pain.

Physically, they were mutually besotted. She had felt fleeting ecstasy before, and even shallow sex had sometimes been as good as the best. Twice before she had believed she was in love. Yet the sex in those relationships had not necessarily been better than in the one-night stands. That had made her confident, unafraid of deep involvement. And so, she was not unrealistically demanding. When those affairs ended, she cried, regretted what she saw as her mistakes, apologized for any pain she had caused, and doubted that she could ever find a suitably happy union.

But Brett shook her foundation. When he hurt, she knew it wasn't her fault. When he shut her out, she didn't feel rejected. When he looked at her with tears in his eyes she never felt that he would fall to pieces or throw her away. But she did feel, and now increasingly while he'd been working on his book, that if she couldn't lessen his pain a little, she couldn't live. It would be impossible to continue, inconceivable that she could find satisfaction without him.

There was no frenzy in this urge to help, because her spirit never seemed to doubt that it held some remedy for him, though it had no name or shape, was nothing she had ever felt for any other person. Perhaps it was simpler than she had ever thought possible: being with him was enough. Nothing supernatural or mystic, just that as long as they were connected, he was safe. It did not occur to her that she was not. She felt no doubt or fear. She was simply facing the present problem, and never again would she be as focussed on anything.

"You're the wordsmith. I don't think I can tell you how much."

His eyes were warm, but his lips disappeared. He finished off the last drop of beer and pushed the bottle and the condiments to one side without looking away.

"You met Robert . . . . ?

"In college. I've known Raul casually for a little over two years, since Robert moved in with him. I keep forgetting the bearded guy's name . . . . oh, yeah . . . Casper. A not-so-friendly bearded ghost. I like his dog, though. Cozy. For 'Cosi Fan Tutte,' the opera. Isn't that cute?"

Brett's eyes never left hers, and his lips came back.

In the sedan parked a block up the street now, Raul was spewing into Casper's face his habitual combination of stern instruction and crude vituperation .

"Moron!"

Robert, listening quietly, had braced himself with his right knee against the dashboard and opened a copy of "The Adventures of Huckleberry Finn." His red hair, neat and full on the sides and unruly in front, the bald spot in the middle masked from view unless you were looking straight down on his handsome head, and a large pattern of curiously flattering freckles, reminded you of Finn. Huck thirty years later, his eyes unexpectedly bright and light when they settled on an open book, though usually shadowed and beady.

Sullen, some would say, unless you knew him the way Jackie did. You might warn people that he was lurking, seeing everything, with wattage turned down so as not to attract attention. And not to show the fear that never slept. Raul was scrunched around halfway facing fat Casper in the back seat.

"You missed, you blind sonofabitch!"

"You tole me to shoot," Casper whined.

"I told you to shoot him. I didn't tell you to shoot at him and miss, fool!"

"I thought that was the signal. I mean, like, you know, the order, right? To shoot now."

"Did I ever tell you the exact second to shoot somebody? Did I? I tell you who to do, and I tell you to do it, okay? And I leave it up to you because you are the trigger man. I am the boss, and you are the sharpshooter. You represent me, and YOU DO NOT MISS! If I could shoot straight, I would do the plugging, but I can't, so I have a lieutenant for this and a lieutenant for that, and you are my lieutenant that shoots. That's what you wanted to be, you told me. You requested, right?" Casper was silent, staring out the window.

"I know, but the movies make it look easy."

"I look at movies too, because they give me inspiration. Right now, I'm feeling inspired to get rid of you."

Robert couldn't stand it anymore. "You are both pathetic, you know that?"

"WE are pathetic? What are you dogface, hairy breath? Slick? Cool? Hmm? You sad he would be alone."

"He was alone when I said he was, which was before you assholes got watching the parade."

Raul's eyes narrowed. Through pursed lips he asked, "Why did we go in there again?"

"She told me to meet her there. And you wanted to meet her, remember?"

"No, I remember I wanted to SEE her. I heard she was hot. I wanted to see the hot widow."

"They're not married. He's married to someone else."

"So? She'll still be a widow: a lover widow, the fuck widow, the romance widow, which is maybe even worse, you know? Losing it all right before you get it all? Ha!"

"Whatever. Anyway, she's my friend."

"Wow! You are setting up her boyfriend. You call ME pathetic?"

"What do you mean, 'setting him up'? Setting him up for what?"

"Aw, fuck, man, gimme a break! Why did you agree to this?"

"You said there was stuff in that guy's book that could fuck up everything. Us."

Raul stared at him.

"Tell me, for Chrissake! What are you saying . . . . . ?"

Still staring out the window, without moving a muscle, Casper muttered through strangely still whiskers, "Robert, Robert, my sweet Huck."

"Like, that I would ever help you hurt somebody for any fucking reason at all . . . . but because he didn't consult you, a complete fucking STRANGER, about his writing? Because he's minding his own business? Unlike you, who thinks his business is YOUR business, because you've got a frigging giant bug up your rear that his fictitious characters are actually real living people, specifically and DELIBERATELY you and me?! Fuuuck! Okay, I swallowed some of that bullshit, and here I am, CHOKING on it. My nostrils are filled with the stench so I can hardly breathe!"

Raul's gaze was steady, expressionless.

"At first, I thought you could get her to get her boyfriend to take that stuff out of the book, or at least disguise it more. NOW I wanna blow my own brains out, for going along with that insanity, this moronic invasion

56

of HIS privacy!"

Raul stopped staring at Robert and looked out the window.

"It's your fault."

"What?"

"You told her about us."

"I told her almost nothing. I never said one word about THAT! Never. She told Brett and he made it up. It was never about you and me, he wouldn't DO THAT. It would be bad for his FICTION to distract from his writing like that. He probably liked that two characters were so so different from each other, like almost opposites, but got together anyway.

Raul's face reddened. "Different?"

"You know, backgrounds?"

"You talking brains? Education? Like, I never went to college, I don't talk real good sometimes?"

"Well, no, I mean, like, you are a real dynamo, a macho business man, ambitious, tough, and I'm . . . . "

"You mean, I'm crude and you're more refined. See? I ain't ignorant. I know some words, too. Maybe it's you rubbing off on me, hmm?"

"I never said anything like that, never. I'm talking about what other people might think."

"How do you know what they think? Because if you say these things to me, you are the one thinking them. Am I right, or am I right? So what did Jackie tell Brett?"

"Brett asked Jackie about my election. She mentioned your name and Brett got excited, she told me. He asked her a lot of questions about our relationship. She told me she thought for a minute he might be jealous of our past connection. She laughed, because we're like brother and sister. He got it. But he kept prying."

"How many times you make All Pro?"

"Two times."

"When I watched you play, I never thought I would actually meet you. I thought you were . . . . you know. And I was twenty years older. Am. And

I never thought I'd find my best friend halfway through my life."

"That's what we are, best friends?"

"Don't you think so?"

"Well, yeah, I mean, sure. You think you're going to die when you're, what, ninety?"

"It's just an expression. They are always looking for dirt. I don't like being disrespected."

"No. Dirt? No, no. What disrespect? He doesn't even know you. He's a journalist who also writes novels. He had a story idea that sounded so similar to ours that he was surprised Jackie was telling him what she was telling him.

"Private stuff?

"No, no. Personality. You know, habits, interests, like hobbies, tastes: food, music, sports. The facts in his story aren't our facts.

"Your habits?"

"Sure. He researches people, then uses bits and pieces to invent a character. Sometimes it's close to an actual person, that's all."

"You believe in coincidences?"

" Of course," said Robert.

"You believe in too close for comfort?"

"Yeah, that happens sometimes."

"You believe in 'THATS TOO CLOSE FOR ME TO BELIEVE IT'S JUST A COINCIDENCE'?

Robert was speechless.

Raul said, "I don't need this aggravation."

"What do you mean?"

"This attention."

"People don't even know."

"But these articles."

"They don't even say anything! Rumors. They're publicity to sell the goddamned book of fiction. Publishers leak innuendos all the time. Speculations from other writers for the book jacket, to attract readers. This isn't real. You made this aggravation. You got a wild idea in your head that fake people in a book are us. I never should have told you."

"I didn't need you! I already heard, remember? This is very real. I can be crazy as shit, but I'm not stupid. Maybe you're in on it."

"In on WHAT? Oh, my god, you mean you think . . . . you think I told Jackie stuff and THEN Brett wrote about it? Goddamit! It's the other fucking way around. I mean, a fucking ridiculous but REAL COINCI-DENCE!! I tell her about our friendship, and she gets excited and tells me that Brett has these two guys who, you know, come from different lives and, and . . . . . hook up, and she says 'what an amazing coincidence,' okay? It's hard for me to believe, too. So, right there, I stop telling her anything!"

"Why did you tell me?"

"I didn't. I mean, you kept asking me, and when I said one of the characters is named Robert, you got hot. Agitated. You asked me the name of the other character. I told you I didn't know. I still don't."

"I bet it's Raul."

"Never. Not in a MILLION years! Oh, fuck! You have to pull yourself together, man. This is nuts."

Casper said, "Raul, you are a one hundred per cent paranoid schizo-phrenic. Hopeless."

"Oh, jeez. I'm surrounded. Now you are pushing it, Casp. Tell it to your dog."

"Robert isn't lying and he's not crazy. You want an explanation, my take on these last three weeks?"

Raul stared at him.

"Your drug is attention. You need to be noticed. You get plenty of attention wherever you go, in your business. You are a big man in a small pond; okay, a medium pond. You earned it. But you crave more recog-nition. Trouble is, we can't always pick and choose where that attention comes from. You got excited when Robert said there were characters in a book that sounded like you and Robert. You were practically giddy."

"I was pissed, man."

"No, you weren't. I've known you since grade school. You're an attention junky. It was only a matter of time before you got the wrong kind of attention from the world, that you couldn't control. You get to keep your friends in line because we like you, and because you scare us. I'm sorry. That's okay. But when you get jittery like this, and so agitated you start threatening your closest friends, I feel bad. Really bad. And really scared."

"Of me?"

"You bet. And so does Robert. And all because you have made up in your squirrely mind a big expose in what might be another best seller from Brett Hemings. The bitch is, you are excited about that. That kind of drama. But you are torn. Afraid of people making connections, but delirious because maybe that is you in a book. It's ironic. Paradoxical."

"Another big word. From another one of my intellectual buddies! I'll give you one: extermination!"

Casper winced.

"You have a small ego."

"What? What the fuck does that mean?"

"Big egos don't get this scared.

"I'm not scared of anything. I'm fucking mad!"

"All anger is fear. You are scared, man. False little egos are fragile. Never mind. You are in a fever right now. You are not making sense. We already went too far. I went way too far. I'm glad I missed. We should just get the hell out of here before it's too late."

"You can go if you want to. We'll drop you off. You think I'm kidding? You think this is a joke?"

"No, I think it's a shame. It could be a tragedy. Maybe it is already. But I have to admit, all afternoon I've been thinking this isn't real. When I heard my own shot, I froze. Scared the shit out of me. It woke me up. I thought, 'What the fuck am I doing here'?"

Robert said, "What shot? What do you mean?"

Raul and Casper both stared at him.

"WHAT THE FUCK IS GOING ON?!"

Casper smiled and stroked his beard. "Hey, Robert. Bobby. You really are Huckleberry fuckin' Finn!"

Raul laughed. "You think I ain't real? The real thing?"

Casper said,

"Oh, man, I know you're real. I just, I just didn't have enough sense to realize that you are not pretending, that you have actually… eliminated people. Man oh man!"

Raul said, "You missed on purpose."

Casper, silent, slowly petted Cozy.

Robert turned almost full around to face Casper. "Eliminated? You mean, killed? Had killed, for chrisake?!"

Casper said, "I'm sorry."

"You bet, good buddy. And I am a sorry asshole for being this blind, man."

Raul said, "You two are frosting my ass. I think I have to let you go."

Robert said, "Are you talking to me or Casper?"

"The dog boy. You too, if I have to."

"Let me go? Let me go? Like how?"

Raul was silent.

"Like where?"

"Like here. Like now, lover."

"Thanks a lot."

"I don't give a fuck anymore. If you're not with me, you're against me. And I can't stand that."

Casper said, "You said there was stuff in that guy's book that could fuck you up. You and Robert. I really care about you. I fucking believed you."

Raul kept staring. "Why did you let me meet her, Robert?"

"I thought if you saw her up close you would feel better about the whole thing. You would not see a scheming bitch in your head. You could get a grip and see a nice woman, my old friend, not some kind of enemy."

"Okay, so she's just an old friend, right? If she's a friend, how come you don't mind putting her lover in this position, arousing my anger?"

"I thought you would not feel so mad anymore once you met her."

"Tell me something, you got a thing for her?"

"WHAT?"

"You maybe jealous of this guy Brett, because she is love with him and not you?"

"Holy shit! You are fucking bananas now."

"You maybe like, secretly hope he might get eliminated so you can make a move on her?"

"Where the FUCK did THIS come from?!"

"Okay, here. Jackie never had much luck with guys. I don't get it, because she is a babe, and nicer than hell. But nobody ever worked out for her. So, yeah, maybe in the back of my mind I'm thinking if you get to Brett and maybe scare him a little he might back off, I don't know, change a few things maybe in the book, even though, like I keep saying, that's just a story, and NOT US; but you you wouldn't threaten him anymore or scare him, and she wouldn't feel bad anymore about telling me things in the first place. And she and Brett might be the real thing. Aw, shit, man, now you've got MY mind all twisted around, so I can't think straight, either! SOMEBODY HELP ME!"

"You got a thing for her, from way back. She loves him, and you are jealous. You don't want it to work out for her. You want the OPPOSITE. For them to break up, so you can maybe…

Robert shot up abruptly from his frozen slump in the passenger seat and said, "Your paranoia knows no bounds. I am almost speechless."

Casper blinked and rubbed his dog's stump, smiling.

Raul continued, "You have a definite thing for her, Robert, an' she loves that schmuck. You are glad that he is in danger, and I am just now getting that you are also a pervert, and you, doggie breath, are a psycho! This is my life here, my reputation!"

Robert muttered, "Othello."

"What?"

"There's a line in a Shakespeare play: 'Reputation, reputation, I have lost my reputation. I have lost the immortal part of myself, and what remains is… Raul's glare stopped him. Then Raul's eyelids closed for a second and Robert spoke the last word: 'bestial.'

"You calling me a beast?"

"No, I mean me. But if you do what you're going to do, you too. But I am through."

Raul's eyes grew large. His lips recoiled. He pounded the dashboard and breathed a long moan. "SHUT THE FUCK UP, both of you! Okay?"

Robert stepped out of the car and slammed the door. He headed back up the street toward the Green Restaurant. Casper exited the rear and slid back into Robert's spot in front.

Raul stiffened, seething. "What are you doing? You don't sit up front!"

He pounded Casper's shoulder with his open hand, then a clenched fist. Casper gripped Cozy tighter, staring straight ahead, trying not to look at Raul. Raul shoved Casper with his palm. Cozy growled. Raul's eyes flashed. He hit Casper's chest with both hands and inadvertently struck Cozy. Cozy whimpered.

Casper protected Cozy with his left arm and shoulder. His right hand brought up the gun to his lap, under Cozy, pointing it at Raul. Raul was breathing hard and moaning, as if hurt. Casper smiled and said, "Drive!"

"What-the-fuck?!"

"DRIVE," and shoved the gun barrel into Raul's hip.

In the restaurant, Brett tilted back onto the vinyl headrest in his booth, with a bottle of beer in his hand. "I like vinyl."

"What?"

"I like vinyl. It's friendly. Old-fashioned. One of the good old traditions."

He closed his eyes and disappeared. Jackie lay her head on his shoulder and closed hers, too. Their hands met in his lap and intertwined. After five minutes, without moving, he muttered, "I'm going out there."

She thought he was awake. When she snuck a look at his face, there was no expression, and his eyes were still closed. Talking in his sleep, she thought. "Sure you are."

Without budging: "I mean it. I'm going to face my music."

"Face your music?"

"Yeah, the music the band was playing. I hear it now."

"Is it funereal?"

Jackie was frightened. And a little excited. She sat up, yawned, and suddenly slammed him hard in the shoulder with both hands.

"Ow! What's that for?"

"What for? WHAT FOR?! Dumb cluck! Don't kid like that. And if you're serious, DON'T BE!"

"I mean it."

"Let's call the cops."

"About what?"

"About those lunatics. Tell them we need protection."

"From what?"

"From those killers."

"How on earth do you prove THAT?"

"We tell them about the gunshot."

"Then the details of this whole idiotic sordid stranger-than-my fiction mess?!"

"They won't arrest them. They'll arrest us."

Jackie was in no mood to argue, no mood to cooperate, either. The tension launched a wet laugh just over Brett's shoulder. He brushed off the imaginary shower with two fingers and stood up. Jackie stiffened, stood up, and placed her hand on his back. He froze momentarily, then stepped toward the front door.

"I'm leaving. I'm out of here."

Without glancing back at her: "No, babe. Stay put. I'm going out alone. I think Sam is parked out back."

64

"I know she is."

"What do you mean? How do you know?"

"You're such a doofus. I love you. But you don't deserve either one of us. Go ahead. I'll tell her."

"What the fuck?!"

"Just go. Let's get this whole shitty melodramatic opera, carnival, nightmare wrapped up. Shut down. Behind us."

Brett laughed and shook his head, dropped his chin to his chest, threw up a backward fist with his left hand, and pushed open the restaurant door.

Jackie was out in the back alley by then. The pickup truck was waiting. Sam and Jackie talked.

As Brett started up the street, he saw the pickup truck crawling along the side from behind the restaurant. He saw Sam gripping the steering wheel with the rigid forward tilt familiar to him as Sam on a mission. Fifty feet beyond the truck, up the street, Robert was striding toward them at a fast clip. Behind him, about a hundred yards, going the other way, Raul swung a screeching u-turn and headed back toward them, scraping the curb.

One street over, across from the front of the restaurant, the band reappeared, still silent, but led now by a barking drum major, the only sound. Leading him and the musicians alongside was a camera truck, moving slowly and impressively in reverse as it shot over the drum major's head at the long phalanx of musicians. He suddenly realized it was a movie crew. They had passed in front of the restaurant earlier pantomiming, making no music, following silent commands from the drum major. Sound would be dubbed in later. He wondered what the music would be. His heart was beating in his ears now. As Brett walked on, Sam's pickup glided into a parking spot across the street. Behind her, Raul completed his u-turn and was now bearing down on them.

Robert spotted Brett and started to jog toward him as Jackie caught up to Brett from behind the restaurant.

Raul gunned the sedan toward them. Out of the alley across the street, in front of him, the band was just emerging onto the restaurant street.

Raul was startled. Sam in the pickup pulled out from her parking spot. Jackie, skittering fast in her stilettos to reach Brett, slammed into his right shoulder, grabbed his left arm and swung him around in one skillful pirouette back toward the restaurant door. Raul tried to avoid hitting the band members emerging from the alley to his left. Purple and gold uniforms blurred in his vision as they scattered over hedges and tripped over one another trying to avoid the vehicles.

A tuba player and two trumpeters later told investigators that they saw Raul and Casper shouting at each other as the sedan careened against the curb and sliced part of a hedge. Robert, running now, made it to the door of the restaurant. He shouted to Jackie and Brett to watch out. Jackie, holding tight, crashed into the door clinging to Brett as the waiter pulled it open, and all three staggered and stumbled inside.

The sedan was aimed like a black torpedo straight at the trio at the door. Sam had had her sights on it far behind, in the rearview mirror, and now saw it close up only a few feet away through her passenger side window.

Inside the sedan, Cozy, seeking shelter, burrowed down between Casper's legs. Casper's hand slid up over his thigh, sticking the pistol into Raul's waist. Raul felt it, screamed, and swerved toward the restaurant with only his left hand on the wheel as his right elbow smashed repeatedly against Casper's hand to deflect the gun. Another blow struck Cozy hard, who screeched and began to yip incessantly.

Casper, in grief, began to weep. He fumbled Cozy to safety into the back seat and begged Raul to stop the sedan. Raul aimed it at the door of the restaurant, where the three had stumbled in only seconds before. Casper grasped the pistol with both hands. Struggling to keep it aimed at Raul, he screamed for him to stop. The gun went off.

Robert had tripped and fallen at the base of the front door. Brett and Jackie had stumbled over him. The sedan headed toward them skidding, tilted at a sharp angle. Sam had a clear view of the doorway and the sedan. Gunning the motor, she aimed the pickup just ahead of the sedan, picking up speed. Her high left fender slammed into the passenger side of the sedan, throwing Casper against of Raul. She heard the gunshot and an agonized "Nooooo!"

The sedan flipped over on its left side and shot straight into the plate glass window. The bullet in Raul's brain had silenced him instantly. The cry of terror and pain had come from Casper, whose regretful eyes were clouded with blood from the ragged wound in Raul's right temple. He scrambled over the body and the seat into the back to cuddle and calm Cozy, spraying spittle and burning tears.

Sam, breathing hard, lay over her steering wheel, the engine still running. Someone had called 911 from the bar, someone else from the band, and several neighbors. Within ten minutes there was a crowd of neighbors and passersby intermingling with musicians in uniform. Movie location trucks slowly appeared at both ends of the street. Several uniformed police officers, assigned to the movie company for traffic control, took over, moving people away from the crashed vehicles and clearing the way for medical assistance which could be heard approaching.

Agitated conversation flew around the neighborhood. Some people thought the whole thing was a movie scene, not just the marching band. A few saw blood and muttered, "Great makeup."

Others, noting the musicians, asked if they had missed the celebration, what special day it was. Sam straightened her long skirt over her cowboy boots, smashed back down on her head her long auburn tresses, secured the mass with her protective straw garden hat, wiped tears out of her eyes and saliva from her lips and cheeks, sprang down onto the sidewalk from her high perch in the pickup, and stomped into the restaurant.

She found Jackie, Brett, Robert and the young bartender and waitress huddled in and around the pink booth. Brett rose to hug her. She stiff-armed him, grabbed a nearby bottle of beer, chugged down half of its contents, wiped her face with the back of her hand, and said, "Thanks for fourteen semi-successful years, lover boy." Brett opened his mouth to speak, but she superceded: "You're welcome." Then to Jackie: "Thanks," and wheeled out with half-empty bottle held high above her head.

The newspapers ran at least six different stories, some just bits and pieces. But at least one version each for the main cast of characters. Business picked up at the Green Restaurant as vegans and global warming worriers came to encourage the conscientious management. Some liked the service and the food. Many were disappointed to hear that the Green Restaurant was called that only because it was painted green, the owner's favorite color. His favorite food was a double cheese burger with a cascade of green pickles and dark green lettuce with green olives circling the four inch high sandwich like the moons around Saturn, known as the green planet. Along with earth, as it happens. Stuck straight through to the plate was an extra long wood pick flying the green and gold flag of The Republic of Ireland. The flag became a coveted souvenir after that day.

Readers who were fans of Brett's previous best seller bought his new book in even greater numbers. Reporters interviewed Jackie and Sam and the workers at the restaurant. No one was willing to say much about the quartet at the table that afternoon or the lone man at the end of the bar. Sleuths sprang out of the bushes. For over a year they followed and badgered all involved. During games, profanities were pitched out to Robert in midfield, along with balled up condoms and chewing gum, and wet used napkins, by pompous fans in the bleachers demanding "the facts." Half empty soda cups and cans flew at him outside eateries. A few cries of "Fag!" and "Closet Queen" struck new notes. Robert pretended to hear none of it. And no one ever threw a punch.

One popular Sunday magazine article went into detail about the making of the film, and how the real life drama that interrupted it was more interesting. Truth not only stranger than fiction but more explosive and bloodier. Sports writers, as expected, had plenty to say about Robert. He had a good year, despite the distractions. His stats were good enough once again to warrant his selection to the All-Star Team. No intimate secrets ever appeared in print, and self-styled virile fans concealing similar secret lives smiled and sighed with relief.

Jackie told Brett she had been talking to Sam almost every day since the rumors began three months earlier. Brett told her he was grateful, but the news gave him a stomach ache, and a worried mind. A handful of television journalists tossed around the scuttlebutt touching Robert and Raul. The business community mourned the tragic premature death of a dynamic business entrepreneur. No salacious details emerged of his private life.

Both Sam and Jackie had good reason to resent Brett, whose self-destructive behavior threatened their lives as well. He was unworthy of their support. Their rueful devotion to him both satisfied and bruised their spirits. All three relationships, if not unbearable, were forever damaged. The women settled for a prickly peace. Brett slept at night and through every afternoon nap with one figurative eye open.

Jackie had spoken to Sam three times that day. They needed to provide cover and an escape plan. It had seemed to work, despite unimaginable drama and unanticipated clamor and bloodshed.

Divorce and recrimination, separation, reconciliations and rueful acceptance flowed all around them. Battered and bruised, Robert, Casper and Cozy floated and bobbed downstream. Jackie, Sam and Brett wished an impossible return to their former simple deceptions. They established instead a private intensive care unit within which they applied to one another shared regret and time, which eased their pain. Vengeance and resentment hovered in the air. They all hoped this latest scuffle would propel Brett's novel to the top of the New York Times bestseller list.

The suspicion in the minds of both women and Casper and many readers, would be whether Brett knew all along that his characters were actual men who would be aroused to murderous indignation, and literally threaten and actually attempt to silence their best-selling exposer.

Casper was defended by a court-ordered attorney and was acquitted by a jury who believed he had rightfully defended himself and Cozy from Raul's blows in the sedan, and saved lives by stopping the car with a half-hearted fatal shot. A publisher paid Casper a hefty advance for a tell-all book. Casper admitted his infatuation with and crush on Raul, but failed to deliver a manuscript. The publishers sued, but public support for "The friendly ghost and his darling crippled opera dog" and their own tenderness prevented them from nailing him.

Casper bought a tiny condo, where Cozy gave birth to three four-legged cuties, two girls and a boy. Casper found a suitable home for one bitch, and kept "Jackie" as a companion for Cozy. Sam eventually adopted the male. One witty observer said Sam took him in exchange for Brett.

The Game

This wasn't a day he had looked forward to, and he regarded that as a setback. Jock liked to think he was an optimist. He anticipated a good day no matter what the weather, for instance. A young man in a variety store recently had responded to Jock's "Howya doin'?" with, "Well, I could do without the rain."

Jock seldom missed a chance. "Ha! I don't think so. Be glad it's raining. I take it you crave the sunshine. Winter too long for you this year?"

"Every year."

"Well, you know without the wet you ain't gonna have any dry. Or any trees or flowers or anything else you like about the summertime. I suppose you'd like to live in Florida or the Caribbean?"

"I wouldn't mind."

"You might not be happy with the hurricanes. And their flies are twice as big as ours, their mosquitoes, too."

The young man was sorry he'd responded to Jock's first casual question. But Jock left him smiling, with a joke, which he told slowly and carefully, monitoring the boy's reaction to each phase of the longish tale so as to gauge whether to continue. He had embarrassed clerks, housewives, male shoppers in hardware stores, and the senior volunteer ladies down at the hospital thrift shop in the last two weeks since Iris had disappeared.

As he came to the part in the joke where the male stripper lets his giant kazoo spring out through the fly of his tight jeans like an uncoiling python (he told this part with bugged out eyes and in a crouch, half imitating the serpent and becoming a ruddy, muscular leering phallus himself), the boy seemed torn. His eyes flitted to the store's entrance, then over to the manager's door, straight to Jock's crotch, though not deliberately, up to Jock's glittering orbs, and settled, half-closed, on his own hands which were clasped and resting on the glass countertop. He didn't move.

The boy seemed transfixed. Jock paused, braced on the edge of the counter prepared to spin away and out the door or, if encouraged in the least, to look around a minute more and buy a little something. The clerk's red face smiled slightly, his hands unclasped, and his body returned to business. "Thanks for the chuckle. Take a look around, I'll be right back."

Jock knew he wouldn't be gone long, and figured he'd probably come back with the manager, so he didn't stay. Iris shooed him out into the drizzle.

"I know, I know, why do I do these things? Well, what do you care, particularly now Huh? Oh, yeah, that's right: someone has to, and who else have I got? Not you. Not anymore. So, is it gonna be just like all the other umpteen times? You go, but you don't go. You gotta get in the last word, haunt me, like Casper the not-so-friendly ghost." Then came the words he dreaded most, this time from her.

"Then cast me out, Jock-o Boy! Cast me, chuck me, toss, flip, eject my sad old drag-ass once and for all, Sweetheart."

But Jock was a positive guy. No gloom-and-doom jaded youth in a novelty store, no slippery gray sky or sooty rain or pining for the tropics was going to get this veteran down. It's guerilla warfare. "She tried to infiltrate me, godammit! Like a foreign spy or saboteur. No, she's a fucking saboteuse! What in God's name did she want from me anyway? Huh?!"

He got to the bar just as the rain let up. Ralph was in the back, playing cards with Earl. Frank was clerking today. Earl let him have the responsibility once, maybe twice a week. Good for his morale. Ralph held up his right hand to Jock the minute Jock slipped into the room. Jock recognized the "mum" sign. Earl was frozen stiff.

Jock wasn't the only one fascinated by Earl's Zen suspension. Jock tiptoed to a good vantage to check Earl's breathing. All he could ever detect was a peculiar twitch which no one else ever could see. All the guys swore Jock was seeing things or making it up to get them going, until Weebie started seeing it, too.

It was Earl's right earlobe. When you saw it the first time you just knew it had to be nerves. But it never failed. Today Jock figured Earl was over it for the first time in maybe a year. But two minutes into the room, he saw the lobe quiver. Jock wiped the drizzle from his forehead with his big brown checkered bandana. His knees gave slightly as he arched carefully up onto a stool. He wanted to signal with the handkerchief or make a sound, but Earl's power and the buddy code prevented him from interfering.

Jock thought, "Earl's going to win again. It never fails."

"Gin!"

Ralph raised both arms straight up. "One more card, ONE, I swear, and I'm there, but he beats me up! I was right there, jeez. Boy, you are something, you really are. Is this what, a year? Have you lost even once in a fucking year?"

His wide mouth in a snarl, Frank brought his left hand down hard on the table, smacking it with an open palm. The hand holding his cards started down with the same force and deliberateness, but gently deposited the hand face down on the remainder of the deck.

"Ten months and sixteen days, Ralph," said Weebie as he passed between the curtains on the entry.

"Weebie, I was just thinking about you. Could you feel me?"

"Sure, I'm clairvoyant, Jock, didn't you know? Where have you been lately?"

"Most recently, I was bugging a young man in a novelty store and dodging Iris, about a half hour ago, and right now I'm contemplating doing myself in; or worse, taking on Earl in a game of gin."

Earl made a clucking sound as if clearing a piece of food from between two upper front teeth, picked up his full glass of warm beer, downed it in a four-second chugalug, shook his head back and forth like a boxer throwing off the numbing effects of a hard right to the kisser and settled back into his chair, breathing peacefully. Without looking around or up,

"Anybody else?"

"I gotta check up on Frank," and Ralph left the room.

"You still grousing about Iris? Why don't you phone her?"

"Still? Whataya mean, still? It's only been a couple weeks, for Chrissake. Don't a guy get at least a month or so to piss and moan, and then a week or two more to feel even sorrier for himself, say, in silent sadness or melancholy reminiscence?"

"Where do you get this stuff? Jock Stuart, you are one of the biggest phonies and one of the most entertaining people I have ever met. Go ahead, silent sufferer."

"Weebie, I didn't know how much you cared! How long has this been going on?" Jock made a grab for Weebie's crotch.

"Come on, let's see if the sad man can entertain you."

"Entertain this, Mr. Crudité!" raising his peculiarly long middle finger."

"That would be a deep exam, doc."

"You could use one, only ...," tapping his own right temple.

"Okay, okay. Ralph, Frank! A coupla beers here." Then to Weebie, "Whattaya mean,

Phony? You never said that to me before."

"You were never this depressed before."

"Is that supposed to cheer me up?"

"And the truth shall set you free."

"Oh, God, therapy!" glancing around, "or just a little friendly advice?"

"All right, forget it." The beers arrived and both men sipped in silence for a few minutes.

Earl joined them. Jock finished off his beer, Earl savored his.

Jock envied only one thing about Weebie, his diplomas, but not enough to go after one himself. They had first met at a bar just over nine months earlier. Jock had Just started seeing Iris. Weebie and Sara had been married a year. Weebie's clear face was in a book, Jock's was a distorted visage, partially obscured by one of those giant vintage amber goblets. His large fists were gripping the thick stem too hard. It could have been a throat, the high head of foam its gorge rising from the pressure.

Weebie looked half way up from his book and muttered, just loud enough to be heard, "You sure, he deserves it?"

Jock didn't respond. Weebie was relieved at first, because he had instantly regretted the reckless intrusion. He moved one stool farther away from Jock's, hoping the stealthy retreat would ease whatever as-yet-unacknowledged irritation he had caused.

"Don't try that passive-aggressive stuff on me, Mr. Academic."

"Oooh, I had no idea you'd noticed. I admit I was a little presumptuous."

"Yup. And a lot rude."

"Are you this defensive only with strangers, or have you always been deeply insecure and paranoid? I wasn't attacking you."

"No, just intruding. Have you always been in the habit of intruding on the private reveries of perfect strangers?"

"I was trying to help."

"Are you by nature this invasive and kind, or are you doing research for a book? You know, I might prefer to be alone, to mind my own business, which I happen to be pretty good at."

"If you're so private and self-sufficient, why are you making a public display of your pain?"

"First of all, sitting still on a stool in a bar is not making a display. It's a quiet sadness. And secondly, I'm in a dimly lit friendly bar on an especially quiet, unexpectedly drizzly afternoon, hiding my pain." Jock wanted to sound stable and sure, so this rebuttal was delivered deadpan and sidelong, over his shoulder. But even if it meant passing out from the pressure, like a glum baby in a tantrum holding its breath, Jock was not going to let slip the smile that bubbled up to his lips. Weebie's voice was pleasant, strong but warm. Jock still hadn't gotten a clear look at him, but the curly dark red-tinged blonde hair and clear translucent skin gave Weebie a cherubic glow. The old-fashioned wire rim glasses gripping all the way round behind his ears said he was practical and thrifty and announced serious purpose.

Weebie was of medium height, wiry, muscular and graceful, like a gymnast. Jock thought he had seen him in the same bar a couple of weeks back. Funny, though, how he felt he could not have given a clear description if he had been called upon by the police or a desperate relative trying to track him down. He wanted to glare at him now, but his instinct was to remain rigid and distant, lest he appear wounded or weak. He would have summed up, "a kind of athletic nerd."

Weebie's impression of almost everyone was usually more detailed, especially of people who looked troubled. Frequently, explosive, even slightly dangerous types, got his attention. Jock looked as if he had lived, been places, seen things, gathered good stories and told them well. It was drizzling that day, too. Though it was the Happy Hour, the bar was just as quiet. Two television sets were on, one with sound completely off, the other barely audible, broadcasting the first game of the N.B.A. finals. It was Saturday, around 4:00 P.M.

Today, it was the same hour. Weebie tried to let go, but couldn't restrain himself.

"Is he your boss or a disappointing friend?"

"Wow! You are something … it isn't a he, it's a she." He cursed himself silently for blurting it out.

"Wow, is right! You're talking to me!"

"Don't get your hopes up. I'm on the verge of turning hostile to a stranger whose insightful interference and analytical skill are attempting to force me to face my shortcomings well before I have peacefully accepted responsibility for my transgression. In other words, butt out, bub, before I kick your ass around the block."

"Weebie opened his mouth as if to object.

"And," Jock spluttered, "send you to the intensive care unit of the emergency ward,"

"You are a voluble bastard, aren't you? Jock was still, Weebie glared at him, removed his glasses, and leaned closer,

"And Clear, and...eloquent."

Jock's left foot slipped off the stool rail onto the floor, and his body tilted toward Weebie. Weebie backed up, slipped his glasses back over his ears in a deft move, raised his arms up as if to fend off blows, slightly mocking, but mostly serious. "All right, all right! Are you the scariest person you know?"

"No, as a matter of fact, you are."

They sat in silence for at least five minutes, staring straight ahead or at their drinks. Still. Without a word or a glance, Jock reached over with a large upwardly open palm. Weebie took it in his and squeezed.

"Okay." After the duration of the grip grew uncomfortably long, "Maybe we should let go. People could be wondering ...... After another long pause, as they finished their beers, Weebie pushed again.

"Maybe this will send me to the hospital, but I can't help wondering, are you ordinarily this wounded only with strangers, or are you deeply insecure and paranoid?" He had pushed back on his stool to widen the gap between them, far enough to be out of reach of Jock's long arms. "Is it really that bad, or are you faking a little?"

"Sorry. I'm way vulnerable today. Shit! Every day ... these days."

"Okay." Weebie settled back on his stool, gripping its legs with turned in toes, and arching his back to stretch and steady himself, never taking his eyes off Jock. Without looking up, Jock mumbled something about pests and strangers off the street, which Weebie pretended not to get. Then he raised his voice just enough for Weebie to hear.

"Why do you say I'm faking?"

"Because you hide your light under a bushel."

"What?! What's that supposed to mean?"

"My grandma used to say that. You know what I mean. Am I the first one to detect this conceit, or just the first one to mention it to you?"

Jock's cover had always been effective. The 'aw shucks, thanks, but I'm really not that smart,' followed by a shrug, when he was pushed to invariably give the correct answer to a question in class. His self-effacement act worked with most people. His teachers knew better. They let him conceal his sharp intellect. They had no reason to expose him, because his papers were exceptional, despite some pressure from a small group of self-styled outlaws who believed that cool meant cruel, and freedom meant cutting all ties with society, snapping all safety lines, especially to traditional institutions like church and school, and especially to family, setting yourself adrift. Jock played to their feeble egos, winning their approval. He stayed in the good graces of everyone. Safe, he felt.

Weebie was younger but wise, and a natural born friend, so he pressed. Jock had kept everybody happy, with preemptive strikes when necessary. He declared his intention early, to go to college, though he wasn't at all certain he would. He made sure only his teachers saw the essays, and his good grades. When he spoke, he was careful to sound not too bright. It was a way of minimizing the expectations of others. And his own for himself. It kept him from disappointing friends and family. And Iris, he thought.

He was comfortable with the jocks and popular with the "brains," some of whom were also jocks. He deflected any criticism from both camps, between which he passed like a protected diplomat or respected spy. He had negotiated at least two truces between what surfaced as two ideological factions. He had not noticed the clear split before. Partly because each side was a mixed lot. It turned out that there was in each, a majority opinion. One side would likely turn out to be liberals, the other conservative, with a few mixed political personalities. At prom time, one side, the conservatives, insisted that all formal dress be traditional, the other that black sneakers be optional with tuxes and gowns. Jock's compromise was a quota. He persuaded the leaders to draw lots on which were printed four different agreed-upon numbers. There were exactly seventy graduating seniors. Instead of conducting a sure-to-be time-consuming campaign and extra-wasteful long voting period, the four white cardboard lots would read 50, 35, 15 and 10. The students would then be allowed to negotiate among one another in private to select who would wear what. The school principal drew the deciding card. It carried the number 35. Some laughed, a few cringed, and most applauded. Fifty-fifty. Good.

But one more question remained. The juniors numbered seventy, but some of them would be dating boys and girls from other schools. Theoretically, the total number could be double that. Back to the drawing board. Jock called a meeting. Three teachers, the principal, four students and Jock concluded, after three hours of debate, that all the fuss had been unnecessary. They decided to let every senior set his own dress code. Two teachers and one student wanted to prolong the hearing by debating the standards for "decent," but Jock pounded the gavel three times, laughed, and declared the decision final and the meeting adjourned.

At the prom, sixteen boys and eight girls wore black athletic shoes—mostly high-top—and one girl tested the patience of the arbitrators by waltzing in, literally, dramatically holding up her gown high enough to flaunt the infraction by wearing black high tops laced in pink, which matched an extra-wide pink ribbon threaded abundantly throughout her woven fat hair.

Jock saw his efforts as a victory for diplomacy, but he also recognized a wasteful effort on his part for control, a play for attention, a civic fiasco, and a distant wail. Like so many correct conclusions by city leaders, governors, and Congress men and women, the simplest and fairest choice had been the first.

Jock now knew for sure that humans were simply contentious creatures who would argue and debate, demand their rights, insist on the superiority of their ideas, exhaust themselves, get bored, and give up. It wasn't compromise. It was simpler than that. The conviction is not important. Only the resistance matters.

The important thing to Jock was that the students graduate. An organized agenda for the prom—dancing, drinks and food, choice of music and perhaps some modest professional entertainment, as the budget allowed—was necessary. But a dress code now, after three weeks of haggling, was not only not necessary, it felt intrusive and trivial. Though the fuss had come full circle back to the simple first impulse, students and teachers combined gave Jock special credit for trying, and keeping the peace. Jock could have had no inkling that his politics were beginning to be formed.

Life was a relentless, unending string of negotiations that too often would mean too little and have no value. That the first uncomplicated idea proposed very often turned out to be the best. He had not heard of Occam's Razor yet, but his instinct understood.

The jocks were a mixed lot. Four were genuine honor students, three were solid students as well as football and basketball stars. They probably had received subtly preferential treatment regarding their grade scores, in order to keep them eligible. No one else knew for sure which ones, if any, and all but one of the remaining nineteen maintained grade points just above the class average. Jock was always respectful, genuinely not judgmental, and always polite. He guarded his privacy and respected theirs.

The "brains" were almost all superior students. Only two could have been called versatile. Most enjoyed playing extracurricular sports, all supported the school teams. None was a top athlete. The line drawn between the two groups was pretty much arbitrary, and ancient by modern standards, amounting to just over seventy-five years.

A tribal rift, at the school's inception, drew the mark in the thick early twentieth century dust of Darwinian unnatural selection, and the rivalry proved so stimulating and entertaining that it thickened and spread like a great faintly forbidding oak thrusting up gnarled and tenacious roots, which had tripped up and caused to stumble too many long-forgotten insecure adolescents. Jock's class, the new breed, felt the instability of a student body stumbling across such lumpy ground. But only Jock seemed aware of the phenomenon.

Why wouldn't the troglodytes long to be smart? It wasn't likely that the brains wanted to dumb down, just to be accepted. Accepted by whom? Which group? Why would any one of them feel the need to be labeled one thing or the other? Did the uninspired non-academics wish to be accepted by the jocks? Or, whose acceptance did they seek? What was the root of such widespread insecurity? Humans. Human nature. Herd instinct. Inferiority complex.

He was a hybrid. He understood. Thesis: Scholar; Antithesis: Athletes;

Synthesis: Jock (jock-brain with an undercover name). Many now, in the Millennium, wanted reconciliation, to belong, to be one or the other, while a few longed to be regarded as both.

Both camps felt the chill of alienation. They experimented with Facebook and Twitter and Snapchat. Some giggled with excitement. Some sneered and reluctantly fired off mini-rocket insults. Some began rating fellow students, trashing girlfriends and boyfriends. Too many found the anonymity titillating. Secret resentments could be spread across the city, the nation, as you hunkered down in your bunker in your pajamas and flipflops, and chirped like a deranged bird.

Few realized they were indoctrinated. By themselves. Instead of merging, two distinct sides with distinctly counter notions were coalescing, each a monolithic gang facing the enemy. Some sent out silly jokes. Some saw the danger of increased alienation looming. Not many realized they were joining cults and gangs, but it was too late. Too attractive. The fix was in.

They were members. They belonged. The delusion was potent, the self-deception frightening. They thought they wanted to find the similarities, the bonds, not the differences. But the differences were more attractive. Toxic. They had hoped for friendships within the system, but found conflict easier and then more satisfying. Jock liked being accepted, but felt apart from both sides. His charms shielded him from both official and casual probes. Integration, cooperation. But secrecy was key.

The bottom line was surprising, but it would hold true and serve his purposes. People want to argue immediately upon hearing a contrary view, but as soon as they have expressed opposition or outrage, they settle back and abandon their point In most cases, opposition and self-assertion are satisfying enough. Convictions turn out to be shallow, and easily abandoned.

He spoke but kept his secrets. He was involved but kept his distance. He was frank but conversed with finesse. James Joyce's "silence, exile and cunning" were his watchwords. Only one person, as far as he could tell, had penetrated his cover before. But Iris was gone now. Not for good, he hoped. He had never felt such loss before. Silence, for now.

Before he stopped going to confession, when he was fourteen, he would walk across town to Mount Carmel, where no priest would recognize his voice in the confessional, because at Holy Rosary, fifteen blocks away he had been baptized, received First Holy Communion and been Confirmed all in the same year. A crash course, instigated by his mother's death.

Exile.

The sudden early loss—she was only fifty-one—lit a redemptive flame at the family altar. They abruptly realized they had neglected Jock's Catholic bondage. Their conviction had always been weak, and now they were frightened and felt guilty. What would the heavenly tribunal make of a heathen child left floating around the planet without the tethering protection and strength of a mother, who was by no means a devoted practitioner, to guide him?

Ten years old, and a semi-orphan—notwithstanding four older siblings perfectly situated to be surrogate parents—and still with a father, although stunned by his loss and like all the rest not actively religious, who remained a properly attentive, though emotionally distant, parent. It was an understandable over-reaction, superficial but well-intentioned, that would cloak his spirit like a hair shirt. Naive. But cunning.

Visits after sunset in a small Midwestern town behind the church to a backdoor residence for priests, to receive "instruction", were dreary. From Father Valentine. Honest, that was his name. Quiet, kind and cordial, he droned. He tried to make sense of peculiar beliefs. He taught prayers. He parroted dogma. He indoctrinated. He shepherded the little lamb. The lamb was polite in return and baaed back, and later cooperated when all the rites were performed upon him to shape a good Catholic boy. The efforts had an opposite effect. The little boy wondered and worried. And sinned. It had been too late.

Across town, he cunningly got a thrill confessing. Not that he was completely honest. He often padded his sin count in order to get a stiffer penance. Sometimes he increased the number of less salacious mortal sins in order to compensate for leaving out embarrassing kinky practices. That way, he felt he was racking up sins enough to show him guilty, all right, and subject to damnation, so the priest hearing his confession would have a worthwhile case against him worthy of punishment and deserving absolution.

The thrill of vulnerability as he bared his soul was thrillingly topped by a sense of relief that flowed over him like a high warm wave as he mumbled the last words of the last prayer just before exiting the shadowy cubicle in which he knelt, rendering him pure and elect again. If a speeding truck ran him over just outside the church, he would fly straight up to heaven. But five minutes out on the sidewalk, the first of a habitual wave of dirty thoughts stained his newly cleansed imagination, and he was restored to normal sinfulness, as promised by the church. First, anonymity. Second, embarrassment. Really. He doesn't even recognize your voice, right? Humiliation because the kinks are too kinky and vile? Third, pure again, as the driven slush. Then, bam! Out on the street, it all flies up like exploded dust and debris scattered by a land mine: pieces of flesh and bloody bones, the perverse Catholic saintly satyr boy.

He had his adrenalin rush when he sinned, then when he confessed, when he pretended to be a bigger sinner than he was, a fourth when he heard the severe penance, a fifth when he completed the litany that made him pure again as a newborn—that was the most intense—and finally a coda to the series of thrills when one tiny "impure" thought released him from all that bondage by restoring him to the state of ordinary sinner, to the normal natural human condition of mild-to-severe guilt and moderate day-to-day fear, released from the pressure to be good, to be sorry, to feel guilty all the time, and to be perpetually under orders, and scrutiny. New freedom, once a week or so, from eternal bondage. Free to sin again, to repent, to be released. Sin was negotiable. Released from prison on a weekly furlough. The Catholic Merry-Go-Round in the Church Carnival. They used to be held in the piazzas of Rome and Assisi, now they set up tables in the parking lots, with crude plastic crosses and crucifixions and madonnas and saints. And spaghetti and meat balls on soggy paper plates.

Purity must remain impossible to attain. Or the show would end.

The collection plates and baskets would be empty, stacked in the corner near the Holy Water basin. The Catholic church sets us up to fail, then we repent, and they come up with a way to let us off. But it doesn't. The not-so-merry merry-go-round: sin, repent, sin repent, repeat, repeat, repeat. It only made him dizzy. Unreal. From the bliss of childhood ignorance, real and safe, to dizzying obedience, false and frightening. At fourteen he risked excommunication, and became real again, and free, free for the first time. From the blissful sleep of childhood to this sudden awakening. And reality rushed in.

Reality was pain and joy, sex and politics, sensual earthly delights, fear, love, betrayal, cruelty, kindness, promises kept and promises broken, and death. No resurrection, no sin, no irrational denial of earthly urges. No unearthly demands and impossible promises.

""I am a planetarian, an Earthling, not a heavenly host.

"It's the truth, it's akchel, everything is satisfakchel. Zippity doo-da, zippity-a, my oh my, what a wonderful day!" Is life actually a Disney movie?

But what about excommunication? For pity's sake, by whom? Does a committee pass that judgment? How does God know? The angels, no, the saints up there, see you and know you are defecting. So, a meeting is convened to oust you. They just know. But I can always get back in, right? No.

I had already figured out that God did not need my endorsement, doesn't need my permission at all to operate. If God needs my acceptance in order to be whole, God can't be real. A complete perfect being can't be needy. If God is not whole, then God can't be real. But if God is neverthe-less real, and God's grace is given to me only if I cooperate, then it's not very gracious of Him. In fact, it is not grace. Grace, by definition, is a free gift. It cannot be earned or deserved or paid back. That's what makes it Grace. Grazie. Gracias. Thank you.

"I will no longer support that in which I no longer believe...." James Joyce again. I believe in sense. Our great claim to fame is intellect. Thought. Reason. If God doesn't make sense, how can God be perfect? Logic is re-quired. Logic tells me that all I need to be in God's good grace is to exist. God made me, and, by God, God had better take care of me! Because I can't.

Does a babe in arms need to believe in the embracer to ensure that the embracer will protect it? Does the baby dangled high above the ground ever fear being dropped, or is it blissfully unaware of any danger? Protection and aid are guaranteed by God mom, and God dad. True then. True when you're ninety-three.

No ritual, no avowal, no praying words required. Generous God unselfishly, unqualifiedly, makes and protects selfish man. God is the pilot. No co-pilot. The genes, God-given, the subconscious, God-given, mom and dad, God-given, place of birth and all influences there, God-given; clearly all, all bestowed and regulated by the grace of God. God rules. Or not.

Not.

They should have taught me that the freedom I needed was freedom from my own will, freedom from my desires, my selfish acts, my insistence on controlling the uncontrollable, which was almost everything swirling around me, and within.

I am God's instrument, God's will itself, yet they told me I was free. Yes, but only free to do God's will, if there is God. They lied to me.

If God is, I am free. If God is not, I am free. On my own. Subject to the slings and arrows, the tides, the seasons, and the sun's rising and setting. If the cosmos is God's creation, and the cosmos operates according to God's will, and I am a part of the cosmos, then I can operate only according to God's will.

FREE WILL to know that I DO NOT HAVE FREE WILL. PHEW!!!

I accept my freedom to think, I accept the results of my actions, I reject supernatural orders. I try to express myself in life and in art as openly and freely as I can, using for my defense the only weapons I allow myself to use: silence, exile and cunning. J. J. Yay!'"

Jock felt alone in his resolve most of the time, but Iris on tiptoe entered his bubble without ever challenging his code. She never doubted his conviction. She never felt him waver. She shared his clear outlook, but knew that Jock harbored a fear that his unleaded, unadulterated crystalline resolution might develop cracks. What would it take to help? What might give him more confidence in what he saw so logically and felt so purely.

She decided to run away. Iris was not the brightest girl in her class. But she was the voice of reason. Iris was the big sister to a shy sister, Shannon, age nineteen, and a spark plug big-for-his-age brother, Acer, twelve. When she helped them, they responded. They were grateful. She was glad. When she coddled them, however, they sometimes balked. She was sad then. Iris knew instinctively that free will meant freedom from her own will. Classic ancient wisdom? Old soul. Just lucky, she reckoned.

"What do you want from him, Iris?"

"I want him to miss me."

"You know he does."

"I want him to hurt."

"Suffer, you mean."

"I guess."

"Why? You love him, right?"

"I do. And he loves me. But he plays this game. He sets you up with a joke, but leaves you dangling. Frustrated."

Shannon brought Iris her tea, in her favorite cup: an extra-wide, flared red bowl with an extra-large handle big enough to accommodate all five of Iris's fingers. The inside was a field of white and red polka dots. They reminded both sisters of the field of early tulips in their grandmother's back yard. When Iris stared down into the warm tea, she saw the tulips in the mist. They were sitting in Grandma Steiner's back kitchen overlooking the broad green lawn that sloped down to the wide strip of black loam along the stream where the tulip bulbs were restoring themselves after a joyful display a few months earlier. Iris was self-conscious at first about discussing her relationship with her teenage sister. But, Shannon was easy to talk to. And she had broached the subject a year ago when Iris sobbed in her arms that she was afraid of falling out of love with Jock.

The confessional that followed and the relief that Iris felt were a secret they would keep for the rest of their lives. Shannon welcomed her own unexpected disclosure. It began as a generous, nurturing act of compassion and encouragement, and swelled involuntarily into an unburdening she had not recognized until she felt Iris trembling in her arms as she pleaded for the courage to accept Jock as is and their marriage as ordained and promising.

Iris had no idea that beautiful, demure, shy Shannon had had until a month before, weekly conjugal afternoons and intermittent evenings with a handsome middle-age pediatrician who had been a friend of the family's since before Shannon was born.

Shannon's account was cool but glowing. She described blissful hours in each other's arms. Her sexual satisfaction exceeded any descriptions in the classic novels and pulp fiction she devoured in her notably solitary hours-on-end in her grandmother's garden and her attic bedroom. Shy Shannon, Iris's temperamental opposite, was fully and shyly and with impressively deft discretion living her life to the fullest before the world had issued her a ticket to ride. Shannon in her way was as instinctively certain as Jock that the world did not hold the keys to any kingdom, that the kingdom was hers and his and Iris's to have as a gift, a beneficence. No apologies. Free. Grace is bestowed upon the individual just because he or she is …here.

"Where is Jock now?" Shannon asked, as they sat sipping tea.

"I don't know. Maybe with Eubie. Yeah, probably.

"Have you asked people?"

"Sure. Not many, though. Sure, he usually asks Eubie what to do."

"Like you, asking me now? How anxious are you? You're unhappy. And scared, right?

"Yes, I guess so."

"You guess so?"

"Okay, I was afraid at first that maybe I was mostly the cause of his unhappiness. But I don't think so anymore. Then I realized that I wanted to hurt him, punish him, for making me so uncomfortable."

"Making you uncomfortable?!"

"Okay. I think I get it now. I supported him, he felt better, but he couldn't get over his fear and indecision

"And?"

"Aaaand, I was upset because he was still worried."

"And …."

"And that means that I'm not enough for him. I can't solve all his problems."

"Well, you mean, this one."

"And, okay, okay, and because I want him, yes, to want me, NEED me."

"Even though you say you're not enough to repair every single thing that's broken in him. What about you? Does he fix you? Does he make every boo-boo better? Listen, toots, you want to talk about Jock's indecision? His indecision? What about yours? And you said you were worried about him. So, what do you do? You run away because you can't fix him, and by running away you break him up even more. Then, you are upset because you're not god-almighty-good enough to make everything better for him. BUT your main concern is Jock, not your own piddling self?! Please! Am I supposed to swallow that? The old game." Iris questioned,

"The old game?"

"Yes, the game."

"Jock enjoys the game when he's not in it. He enjoys watching others squirm. He's not mean. He's a voyeur. Oh, he gets a kick out of fixing things. People rely on him. He always liked that. He means well, but he needs the credit, too. But when he's on the other end, he panics. You knew that."

Iris sipped her tea, staring at Shannon, and drumming the table with all five fingers of her left hand. Shannon stared back, sipping too, from a green cup the twin of Iris's except for the color, and cradled in both hands.

"Simple as that, huh? My god, how do you know all this?

"Old soul, I guess. Plus, Ron. Doc Larsen. Daddy Lover."

"Mmm, wow! That is still making me woozy."

"Can this be fixed?"

"Maybe. Probably. What do you want?"

"Jock. And peace of mind."

"Okay!"

"You think you've scared him enough by now?"

"I think I am more afraid than he is."

"Good."

"How is that good?"

"Now maybe you'll stop trying to change him and yourself."

Iris and Shannon spent the week together. Iris didn't want Jock to know where she was yet, but Shannon sent word to Weebie, who told Jock that Iris was working it out and would get in touch with Jock and come home soon.

Jock started his application to Western State. Weebie hugged him and cheered. He told him Iris would jump with the same joy. Jock cried.

"Oo-ooh! I didn't know you could CRY! People hiding under bushels hide their tears."

"How in the hell do you know all this?"

"I don't know. Old soul? No, I've played this game before."

The Ballad of Bobbie and Mack

"I'm shorter than I look," Bobbie was saying to her customer. She asked his name and smiled.

"Eli."

She gripped the thread between her teeth on the left side of her mouth. Lipstick spread above the natural line made a scarlet bow of her upper lip. Her nubby fingers, the nails a glossier red and one shade brighter than her lipstick, looked to Mack like a cartoon crab gripping its prey, as she snapped the thread and straightened the cuff of the jeans in her lap in one smooth motion. Her mouth twisted and her crimson lips pursed as if to devour it. Mack had seen the gesture every day for six years. It still aroused him.

There was no shyness in her, though Mack knew a quiet side. Rich color overwhelms most people. Bobbie could wear the boldest prints and rudest hues. Yellow with red was her favorite combination. Same as the colors Michelangelo used in the uniforms of the Swiss Guards assigned to guard the Pope at the Vatican in Rome, she liked to point out". I'm a heathen, but the priests don't know it, and I appreciate art."

"Why is that?" Mack shouted from the parlor.

"Why is what?" said Bobbie as she lined up and pressed together both pants legs on the ironing board.

"What? I didn't hear you," said Mack.

Bobbie suggested he open his ears or move closer, if he wanted to discuss optical illusions. So he parted the Beverly Hills curtains and leaned in, enunciating very slowly and with prissy exactitude: "Why . . . are . . . you . . shorter . . . than you look?"

"Because I...am...long-waisted. She hissed all of this past the needle clenched in her crab mouth. When I'm sitting, I'm just as tall as you." Resuming her sewing: "Your long legs make you tall when you're standing. My long torso makes me tall when I'm sitting, tall as you. Ha!"

Mack didn't speak, but kept his eyes on her, scrunching back one panel of the frayed curtain with a big fist. He did not see the new customer.

"Are you staring again?" "Whattaya mean, again?" "You know. Exactly." "Yeah."

"Yeah you know, or yeah, you are, or both?"

"Yeah."

"Keep your eye on the stew." Bobbie's stew was the best dish Mack had ever eaten anywhere, and he'd been around the world sixteen times, he wanted you to know. This was the day he'd tell her he wasn't leaving anymore. "Hey, I said check on the stew."

"I did, it's fine."

"Why didn't you say so?'

"I did . . . to myself. Just not to you."

"I don't have telepathy."

"Like hell you don't!" Bobbie laughed her brash cackle. Bobbie worked in the front corner room, just off the enclosed porch. She sewed. She called it stitching the world back together, piece by piece. You could see the kitchen through the drapes, gray and wine colored, the wallpaper pattern of large green leaves peeking out from under enormous yellow flowers stabbed in the middle with sassy stamen. Hibiscus, maybe. The dark blood background and the lighter trim, satiny and bright, gave the walls an elegance and a memory of richer times. Maybe they were bought by an admirer long ago. Maybe they came with the house, that's all, when I got it. Two kitchen walls were baby blue. "They match my eyes."

Bobbie had those half glasses on the tip of her nose and knew how to look up without looking up, and could reach for tiny scissors and needles without letting go of the cloth, usually pants cuffs or shirt sleeves, sometimes zippers and hems or buttons of skirts and dresses. Mostly men's clothes, though. And only men ever sat in her kitchen. Her eyes were bright as the sky. Lipstick gave her an upper bow lip higher than the natural sliver she bemoaned. The lower lip jutted out naturally like a tiny crimson tray asking for something to be put on it.

"Mack!"

"I know, I know, the stew's doing fine."

"You do have telepathy, see? Stir it and make sure no potatoes are sticking." All of this through her clenched teeth past a trapped needle like a paused harpoon, out of the right side of her mouth. Her fingers pressed the cloth of a new zipper between folded-over edges of wool that formed one side of a pants fly. She squinted and grimaced as if applying English to the maneuver, squeezing the fabric top and bottom to make a sandwich that would hold the zipper's membrane steady and straight to take the sewing machine's hard-jabbing needle. Her foot controlled the old-fashioned trestle like a ballerina's heel-and-toeing the stage. Mack's eyes seemed to be on the nearby television, but his glance slipped out from under his lowered lids like a spying child's peeking out from under the grassy edge of a pup tent. He smiled and grunted, and sighed almost inaudibly.

"What? Did you look again?"

"Whatta you mean?"

"There you go again. The stew!"

"Oh, yeah, twice already. Yeah. It's good. No sticking." He hadn't budged since the last look-see. Bobbie finished the zipper, caught the thread between her teeth and yanked. Her knuckles were slightly thickened from creeping osteoarthritis. The added enlargement gave her hands a curiously ominous authority, not at all unattractive. There was no pain, just surprising extra strength.

Mack raised his voice to carry over the steady hum and intermittent click-clack of Bella's sewing machine: "I told you I decided, right?"

"Decided what?"

"I didn't tell you?"

"Would I ask, if you already did?" "I've decided to stay."

"Stay . . . . where?"

"Here in town. To not travel anymore."

"Really? Why?"

"I can think of lots of reasons." "Give me one . . . or maybe two."

She said this past thick blue thread held all the way across her wide red lips, one arm holding out another trouser leg to full length, the other gripping and pulling tight the crotch of a pair of holely, faded jeans. Staring through a gap in the curtains, Kurt saw a bloody fish's mouth on a line. His groin stirred.

"I don't need a reason."

"Yeah, but you always have one."

"I like it here." There was silence for more than a minute, stabbed by the droning sound of the sewing machine.

"Check the stew again, one more time, wouldja? Turn it off, maybe. I bet it's done. Go ahead and taste, should be the way you like it."

He was on his way after the first directive. From the inglenook, he sidled past the flowered drapes like a man on a dance floor lightly but pointedly jostling his partner. It was his prowl, when he was aroused.

Mack had been in love before, or thought he had, but never like this. So, this may be my only time, right? The thought had occurred to him at least once a day in the last six months. He started sleeping there on and off from the first week six years ago, but alone. After a month, he had become Bobbie's bed mate most nights, but never objected when she said, Not tonight, Sweetness, and smiled goodnight and fell asleep. Mack would wrap himself up in the large wool blanket on the giant easy chair just inside the front door or retreat to one of his caves. He said he was a commando who goes on raids, his daily mission to wage guerrilla warfare in a hostile but manageable world. He called his room near the beach his headquarters and Bobbie's place his port in a storm. In his poems, a fairy queen mother came to comfort children. But she frightened men.

Bella's house on Marine Lane wasn't Mack's only pad. He spoke of several to Arty at the Fire Station on the corner, and to Reg, who owned the friendliest bar in North America, according to Mack. The Piccadilly Pub on Ocean Avenue. One of his coziest hideouts was the tiny bedroom just off the storeroom behind the bar, which he could enter from the brick-paved alley in back, that ran along the parking lot. You could see the beach from the high window if you stood on the bed, and get a perfect view of some spectacular sunsets. He wrote most of his poems there. So far, he had read them only to his boys. Only one to Bobbie.

Three days a week, Mack attended classes at the community center nearby. He couldn't get a degree there, he explained to people who asked, but he could earn certificates, just like frequent flyer credits, but which converted to a degree at Beachfront Community College, which would be a good enough credential for a substitute teacher position there. At his age? Who'd hire a battered old vet like him? And who'd be stupid enough to be tied down like that at his stage of life? Besides, Bobbie came first, as long as he toed the line and wasn't sloppy.

Bobbie hated disorder and rudeness. In anyone, but particularly in grown men. She needed her men and her home to be comfortable. Cooking and sewing were her life, but could she be cheerful without men? " I am an Armenian-Irish girl with ballet slippers on her toes, eyes in her fingers and Tinkerbell on her ankle. And in her heart." Her words. Swear to God.

This was her woven life. "I darn it, like the socks, and I patch it up all the time, like the jeans." Her Den of Iquity, she called it, when she said her prayers on her knees at night, elbows on her bed She left out the men, mention of them, I mean. There, and in conversation. What you leave out is probably what is most important. If you admit it to everybody, it's exposed to harm. She accepted gifts, money included, but not in payment, only in tribute. If it was sincere. She would not earn a hundred dollars more in a year if it hoisted her into a troublesome tax bracket. She offered a comfortable waiting space, cheerful surroundings, home-cooked stews, and unbreakable thread. Her buttons never fell off, and her skirts and jeans never frayed.

She needed stability, but she enjoyed surprises. This balmy California day was fixing to stir up more than her pot of stew.

"Tony and Jack said you could fix anything on a pair of pants. They said you know best what needs to be done, so do it, okay?" Bobbie winced at the over-familiar directive, but was warmed by the incongruous, innocent tone. The voice was deep and velvety, grown up, seductive but childlike, with a whippoorwill in it. When she looked up she saw black eyes under shiny curls capping and framing a chestnut-colored moon face with the whitest teeth she had ever seen. His smile was expectant, slanted down at her to the left. At first she could not speak. 'His eyes don't have pupils,' her mind said. His wondered why this attractive woman wasn't looking at his fine legs. 'They're too dark to see out of,' she thought. He hadn't yet deciphered her frozen stare as wonderment. Her bright baby blue eyes darkened a shade. Beads of perspiration popped out all over her normally cool upper lip. A tropical breeze both warm and chill raised goose bumps across her bosom and shoulders.

"Who told you . . . what?" "Did I get the names wrong?"

"Maybe. No, maybe not. I know Tony, but I haven't seen Jack in a couple of years. Are they friends of yours?"

"No, ma'am. I just now met Tony, in that bar over there on the beach, and Jack is back home in Minton." Bobbie's gaze remained steady. "Loosiana, I mean."

A stranger might think him cocky and too sure of himself. Eli was confident, was all. He'd been taught by a Creole mother that in the swamp life was rich and never lonely.

Creatures depended on each other, nature was strict, but the rules were clear, understood and fair.

People were not so reliable. They made up rules of their own. Especially in the city. Eli already knew the difference. He was a swamp creature who knew how to find patches of sunlight, could navigate a slim hollowed-out log across cypress roots standing up, poling barefoot. Same thing, his Mam told him, in the city. Only there were more snakes and alligators, not-so-pretty birds and too many hidden roots, sink holes and quicksand. Smiling but wary, suspicious but friendly, he had been cruising the streets of Marina del Rey, Venice and Malibu for a year. Sometimes he recognized other swamp people who had never been out of the city. They had been delivered by mistake to the wrong address. He sensed their discomfort. Many people in the city were crocodiles, dozing in the muddy gutters, snapping off lunch, or cruising just below the surface in murky waters, beady eyes alert but unfeeling. Crocs liked flamingoes and it was a pitiful sight to see one squawking and flailing, clamped in the jaws of a big twisting monster, feathers flying off like pieces of a soul, drifting down into the streets and bloody muck. Eli could tell the difference between the crocodiles and the flamingoes. He thought.

Mack stood gazing but blinking nervously from behind the flowered curtains. Tall orange, white and tan flamingoes in a forest of huge green palm leaves with accents of burgundy and mustard on the edges of leaves held on thick black stems against a pink background gave the kitchen and Bobbie's workroom a South Seas air. She liked telling people this was the paper on the walls of the famous Polo Lounge in the Beverly Hills Hotel. It wasn't exactly, but she knew it wasn't likely that anyone entering her sewing room had ever been to the Beverly Hills Hotel, so what's the harm.

Mack's golden brown skin and gray temples, his cantaloupe biceps, veiny wrists and catcher's mitt hands reminded his shipmates in Hawaii of King Kamehameha. Holding back the tropical drape from atop his six-foot-four frame, Mack might have been one of those statues of the warrior king dotted around the Big Island, a mythical god in radiant bronze flesh. He had seen boys and girls irresistible in their grace and achingly innocent, in Bora Bora and Papeyete. They had admired him in return.

Bobbie finished the zipper, caught the thread between her teeth and yanked. Her knuckles were slightly thickened. Arthritis, but not yet painful. The paint on her nails was spotty from wear. The inside of her first two forefingers were permanently yellow from years of smoking Pall

Malls. 'The long ones. No filters.' She quit ten years ago, and didn't allow smoking on the premises, not even outside. If she smelled cigarettes on your breath, she'd wince and glare. Occasionally, she asked a customer to leave, no offense, 'I'm allergic.'

Her fingers spread the crotch flat and caressed it too many times. She would eventually finish it with a hot iron, but her fingers seemed possessed some days. She held up the trousers for a better look, then put them back down and fussed over one edge of the zipper cloth, pincering it first with one, then two fingers.

"Did you do it?"

"Huh? What? Do what?" "Did you get it flat enough?"

"Oh, you! Keep your eyes on the T.V. or I'll flatten you! Turn down the flame on the stew or turn it off and have some. If it's ready." Bobbie's foot left the black iron trestle and rested tippy toe on the gray carpet. Her thin gold anklet with a Tinkerbell charm drooped and sparkled. Mack loved it. He had given it to her on her fiftieth birthday two years ago, saying that ankles as pretty as hers deserved jewelry.

"How special-sweet," and thrust out her tiny dancer's foot. "Put it on, Mackie honey."

When Bobbie called him Mackie, he blushed like a school boy, which he still was. Three years into a comfortable retirement on a pension from the Seaman's Association, he was teaching auto mechanics at the community center near the police station at the beach. That's where we met. We got to talking about Korea, and he told me about the poems he was writing.

Mack told Bobbie that people worried about him. What was he getting out of his life? Mack was touched by their concern. Strangers at the bar and along the beach, and some of Bobbie's regular customers, wondered if he was happy. When he told Bobbie, she groaned.

"Are you nuts? You learn something new every day, you laugh and eat the best stew. I patch up holes and hems. They can't believe you're doing just what you want. They're jealous. You should have a goal? A goal! Ha, like they do? They don't know how to do nothin', not even mind their own business." Mack thought he already had what he wanted. Until today.

That Saturday in early July was exceptionally hot. The lower half of California tends to be dry. Because it's a semi-arid climate, Mack had read. Only one season, that's all you get, though it varies from warm almost always, to scorching hot . In the winter it rains, too hard for a minute, but never enough. When it pours, the roads flood. Planners never thought of gutters.

He was born in Wisconsin, on a lake. Four full seasons. He liked them all, but he hated the summer mosquitoes. They banished him to the house. Shut in, he read, and listened for the robins and jays. And owls at night. He feared for the robins and jays. No one had to teach him to stop and smell the roses. Lilac blooms didn't last long, but they doused you and the air if you brushed up against them or cut them for a vase on the kitchen table. Daffodils and tulips, peonies and irises had no perfume. But they stood up to you, vivid and confidently perennial. Southern California flowers were semi-tropical and decidedly droopy by comparison, but perennial too, and seemingly perpetual, like the endless sunshine.

The sun had turned pale by late that day. But bronzed blonde girls and burned boys glowed in the twilight, some the copper color of a polished penny, heads nodding like the heavy sunflowers in Bobbie's front yard, as they ambled past the bungalow. They had sat on the warm sand since early morning, splashed in the soft July surf, tossed and batted frisbees and balls, wrestled and yelled, stumbled and flailed and spat away sand and salt. Rubbery smooth limbs fumbled in awkward embraces with uncertain intent, grab-assing, risking jittery kisses and hugs. Life in southern California was carefree. The West was young, open, lawless, unafraid. Crimes were mere inconveniences, gruesome crimes cool. Ugliest things were flattered by the light rising off the silica glitter of the beaches. At midnight, dark deeds cast a fluorescent glow.

The light far out on the sea was like that. Leaping off the edge of the horizon at dusk, when it flared up in a final blazing plunge, the sun confirmed the earth was flat. In the low glow left hovering over the marina, Mack was aroused by the waves slathering the pier and humping the hulls. In the twilight, he strolled along in the midst of the golden flock toward the exotic widow's cottage haven .

Cooking and sewing were Bobbie's life. Roberta Dalitian, the Armenian-Irish girl, ballet slippers on her soles, orange polish on her toes, a mole at the left corner of her mouth, a cap of frizzy auburn hair framing a pouty-pretty face, firm pink melons riding a tiny waist, the cheery widow stewing and sewing in the southern California sun.

Mack thought he was Bobbie's cheer. Ralph did, too. They both had worn spots, and she darned up her men each day, she'd tell you, like their socks. Ralph welcomed her insistence and her harlot's hunger. Bill had no doubt that he and Bobbie were a match made in as close to heaven as possible. Bobbie would say the sex was more diabolical. Hot and a little rough. Her den of Iquity, she called her house when she said her prayers on her knees every night.

She asked God to help her truly forgive in her heart the slaughter of her ancestors decades ago, and to understand her needs, overlook her lusts, and note her good deeds. 'I'd be good in heaven, I'd make it interesting.'

The pants were baggy, and torn at the knees. They had no right to look stylish on the scruffy creature next to Bobbie. His looks both pleased and affronted. The vision before Mack seated on Bobbie's frayed silk hassock in a tee shirt and underwear—he imagined— invisible under the extra long shirt tail, matched the prettiest he had seen in the South Pacific. The boy rose in a slow sway, uncoiling. His auburn face flicked a raw-pink tongue from between full bow lips, naturally rosy, that bore a disorienting resemblance to Bobbie's crab mouth. The boy's hooded eyes followed her hands as they measured from his crotch to his ankle. Their eyes met for a second, hers returning quickly to the tape, his gaze streaming past hers in an unblinking gleam as it rose to fuse with Mack's. She gripped the boy's thigh firmly with one hand as she steadied herself to rise, and in the same motion stretched out the other, offering the measuring tape to Mack. The boy's insouciance, the tension in his thighs and the tilt of his shoulders radiated confidence and a warning. When he walked in that afternoon, or glided or floated or maybe just materialized, Bobbie was not ready fifty years, two husbands and dozens of lovers' worth to recognize the species. He was a figment. A genie, or a dybbuk.

Mack appreciated all kinds of beauty. The only difference between boys and girls were a few chromosomes. Eli's muscular legs reminded him of his own. Some of his admiration sprang from his own vanity. Mack knew he was still attractive, but he didn't try to compete with young bucks. He figured that he was probably almost as strong as any of them but knew for sure that he was just as horny.

Bobbie's cottage on Marine Lane wasn't Mack's only pad. He spoke of several to Arty at the fire station on the corner, and to Reg, who owned the friendliest bar in North America, according to Mack. The Piccadilly Pub, on Ocean Avenue. Mack's coziest hideout was the tiny bedroom just off the storeroom behind the bar, which he could enter from the cobblestone alley in back, that ran along the parking lot. You could see the beach through the high clerestory window if you stood on the bed, and get a perfect view of some spectacular sunsets. Lying on the bed that filled the room, Mack could always see the sky through the wide expanse of glass, his panorama of the heavens, he told Reg.

Mack's boys came to him here. Youthful men, really. Always buff, and usually a little shy. Some, maybe a touch backward. Mack was a good listener. And when he spoke, could be mesmerizing. Mostly he asked questions. A room in the groves of Academe. Socrates and Eros. Once, Bobbie called him Apollo. Mack was surprised. "Wow, Apollo!"

"I'm not intellectual, but I ain't stupid. I looked it up. When the Apollo astronauts were all over the T.V., I looked it up. Him. My kind of god, you know what I mean? Super Interesting."

"Your looking him up, or what he was?"

"Both. Hee hee. Choosing that name. Them NASA boys!"

"Nasty boys, too. I've known a couple."

"What?"

"Nothing."

"You'd be surprised how many intellectual grandmas come in that bar, Bobbie."

"YOU would be surprised how surprised I am not. My Nonna Pina. For about ten years, until she went to the home. Needed the attention. The buzz. Never got stinking. Just lit up a little. I miss her."

Mack was everybody's. A housewife's shadowy dad, the surfer girl's funky possibility; any surfer boy's absent rabbi or priest, trainer or coach. He was an easy friend. The only one he didn't seem to belong to was himself.

When Bobbie asked him to finish measuring the boy, Mack was next to him in a couple of blinks, gripping the tape . Bobbie's outstretched hand had passed it off smoothly, like a relay runner, into the closer's big fist.

"Would you mind stepping back here?"

Eli slipped behind the gray blanket that masked the inglenook. At the back was a tiny unused fireplace outlined in shiny black and yellow tiles. Next to it leaning against the wall under a small open casement window stood a dime store mirror, gray spots showing in one corner and along the bottom, where the silvering had worn off the back. The glass was cheap, so it elongated figures slightly, causing a slimming effect. Mack said Bobbie bought it deliberately, not just because it was inexpensive..

"You need me to get this up?"

Mack, already on his haunches at Eli's feet, looked up. "Huh? Raise what?"

"My shirt."

It took Mack a few seconds. As he slid his look up the soft plaid shirt front to Eli's moist grin, he thought what a clear strong jaw and smooth skin the boy had; and a deer's legs, a young buck alright.

"Were you a track man?"

"No, sir. But I walk a lot, hunting and fishing and, you know. Visiting folks."

Eli's hands were still on his shirt tails, ready to oblige, but Mack was up one side with the tape measure and had already slithered around back and had his thumb in the crease of the boy's buttock and thigh. "Don't bother moving that shirt. I got what I came for." Putting out his hand, "I'm Mack."

"Eli," as he took Mack's big paw. He showed no discomfort from Mack's hard grip. Mack knew it had to be hurting a little, but when he let up, Eli's hand did not retreat quickly. Covering up? Standing his ground?

Bobbie from the other side of the blanket: "Did you get it? Him?"

"Sure, hold your horses, okay? He's thirty-one inches, give or take. His left leg appears to be half an inch shorter, though. Give or take. Of course, it could be me who's tilted."

Bobbie said, "You give, I'll take. And I know you're tilted, all right. You can take later." Mack winced, then tingled.

Mack pointed with his thumb: "That's Bobbie, by the way."

"Hi, Bobbie. Is everything all right, ma'am?"

"Sure. Get out of here, both of you. I'll be finished in two minutes flat."

For the next six months, until just after Christmas, Bobbie and Mack shared more days together than they had in the previous two years. They weren't counting. They didn't keep score like their neighbors. This is my private assessment. I have been telling here a friend's tale, a report with a troubled heart. To protect them and preserve the truth as maybe I alone saw it.

They deserve to be defended. Bobbie and Mack never put on airs. In the cottage the climate was fair. Eli's arrival changed the weather. When he started napping in the back room, at first Mack was jealous.

Reg hired him to tend bar. He worked all shifts, whatever Reg offered. Reg developed an affection for Eli that irritated him. Reg was independent, he liked to tell you. Unchained. He had been shackled, as he described it with relish, without a contract, he always emphasized, to a blonde bombshell. She wasn't a witch or a bitch, though his friends thought so, but she clung too hard and 'sucked the sweetest juices out of me.' Trouble was, he liked it. The separation was sad for both, but not bitter.

After eleven years, Rosie actually landed a movie contract. For three years, she appeared in nine so-so films. All small roles. She lost her hour glass figure, held on to her sense of humor, grew fonder and fonder of rough sex, and settled into marriage with a film producer twice her age, had two children in three years, was widowed when they were five and seven, and moved with a hefty stock portfolio, a fully rented fifty unit apartment building in West Hollywood, and a two million dollar life insurance policy, to Rancho Mirage.

Reg was grateful. He sent Rosie a birthday card every year, signed "Thanks forever, Your Reg." Free at last, Reg's mood improved. His famously sunny disposition had dimmed noticeably for the first two years after Rosie had left. One day, Eli slouched through the swinging doors of the jolliest bar, and as if levitating on a shaft of light, glided up to Reg's hunched back as he sorted bills at the vintage cash register.

"Howdy, Reg," said Eli.

Reg was polyamorous, he would tell you. He thought of people as sexual or "not so sexual," when someone shot a label at him. He was impatient of stereotypes and slurs. I liked him. Everyone liked him. And he appeared to like his customers. "Enough," he'd tell Mack, "to keep business flowing." He liked Mack more, and Mack returned the favor.

Mack and Reg were regarded by those who didn't know them as inseparable friends. They hugged each other more than any two men they knew. They kissed each other on both cheeks, usually, and when they hugged, both men would hold on thirty seconds longer than men usually do. Reg would mutter, "Oh, fuck, here!" and peck Mack's lips with his. Mack liked it. Those who liked them both, loved them together.

Reg felt the climate in the bar was changing. The regulars were used to variations in the social weather, as the tourist trade fluctuated. One winter season bikers from Sacramento and San Diego converged along the coast of Santa Monica from the carousel to Redondo Beach. The bar was stuffed with tattooed arms, raunchy boots, sour leather vests, and sweaty wrist bands. A spot or two of cologne in the air raised noses when a lone hunk strolled by. Reg liked cologne on his women. On men, too. He had always liked English Leather. Lately he had detected a lime that lingered and followed him. From the south?

The weather in Mack's cave was humid. It had seemed dry most of the year before. It had been cool and breezy this past winter, balmy and still, this spring and summer. Fall was the referee. The end of the growing season, the mellowing of leaves, the lightening of fruit trees, the strip-tease of maple and Aspen leaves.

Mack was being stripped, too. Of inhibitions that held him in dismissal, arms folded, legs crossed, leaning against the doorframe at the exit of the gym, or the emergency exit of the fire station. While jocks sauntered in and out of the gym and firefighters slouched on and off hook-and-ladders in heavy gear, Mack yearned for contact. Bobbie was full.

Bobbie fulfilled his needs. But not all of his cravings. He didn't always feel longing purely. At his first glimpse of Eli, it was a flash of sunlight in a cool mist. Soothing. But it troubled his mind. Bobbie saw it.

Reg had been fulfilled by Rosie. By her devotion and her gratitude, and her recognition that their life together had given them both what they needed but could not satisfy every desire. Rosie freed them. The perfect storm.

Mack and Bobbie were staring into a glare— or fury—or headwind. Disaster did not suggest itself. A Scirocco? Bobbie never encouraged Eli's advances, but Eli never needed encouragement. He had always been desired. By his mother and brother, the girl next door and next door to her, teachers, coaches, the ministers and their wives. He absorbed malice when it was apparent: warmed, not scorched by it, seemingly oblivious even when it hit him from a flame-thrower. Observers admired his forbearance. It wasn't conscious. Eli instinctively understood the advantage of stoic neutrality. His beauty absorbed the bruises. They increased his glow, and his emotions swelled with added fire. Resentment from others grew in proportion to his spreading appeal.

They smiled and teetered when he appeared. Bobbie said to Mack, "He's got natural grace. Like you, Big Boy. Just different style, is all. You may be destined, like before."

Mack stood still.

Here's where the story gets tricky, tricky because life is like that, and frisky, because some stories want to run off, run in more than one direction, and you have to chase it around to get a grip on it, track it, keep an eye, or rather your brain on it. A song has to be coherent. It can be silly or punny, like "Mares eat oats, and does eat oats, and little lambs eat ivy. A Kid'll eat ivy too. Wouldn't you?" In the pun is sensible nutrition. And resignation. And when real life—that may sound like a song—gets punny all the way to goofy, it too eventually coheres into sense, even when a senseless death occurs. Even a gruesome one.

Bobbie had said "like before" more than once in the last ten years. Neither had ever gone into detail. Mack recalled that almost exactly twelve years earlier a young buck slightly older than Eli had presented himself with equal aplomb and in a similarly seductive manner to Bobbie, with not one but two items that needed mending: jeans severely torn at the left buttock and a shirt ripped almost in two, revealing a superbly muscled body on a tanned lithe frame three inches taller than Eli's. She tried to recall his name. It was a Monday morning in August. The air was thick and moist. The beach was deserted. Cleaning crews were combing the sands, rustling up paper cups, straws and napkins, condoms and plastic forks and knives. Locals with metal detectors were scanning and stuffing trinkets into long cloth shoulder bags. A few couples were picnicking on tiny blankets, relishing the weekday wide open space. Pale sun shimmered on low waves, seagulls squawked and floated and dove for scraps on water and on the sand. Clumps of eerily assorted birds poked and squealed at each other vying for scraps of bread and morsels of food. Seagulls all looked alike. But that day Reg and a few visitors to the bar remarked that "peculiar" birds were "out there."

"Out there," said Reg as he walked down the back alley toward Mack's room. He was with a customer who had volunteered to help Reg straighten up the room. He was a blonde, buff tanned boy Reg enjoyed looking at. He confessed later that he had a vague notion of taking a chance with him in the room. But the boy entered first past Reg's outstretched arm as he held the door wide for him to pass. The boy took one step in and screamed.

Another beautiful boy's body was halfway sprawled over the edge of the king-sized bed. A knotted and tangled thick boat rope was loosely around his neck, but it was not attached to a beam or jammed over the top of a door. A noose was around the neck, but the examination later on did not indicate that the boy was strangled by it. It was red- white and blue, like some seen on the boats in the marina. They tried to trace it to an exact boat, but seawater and sun neutralized any clues. If only ropes had DNAs or held fingerprints! A year ago, just after Eli arrived, Reg overheard Bobbie and Mack quietly correcting each other in a whisper behind the curtain to the kitchen while Eli waited with a lap robe over his knees for

Bobbie to let out the waist of his favorite jeans. Mack said, "Adam." Bobbie corrected, "Abraham." They were Reggie's bar jeans. He made sure regular customers knew he had been wearing the same jeans, unaltered, for fifteen years, testimony to their high quality and his fitness. Now, at long last, his belly forced a minor alteration. Reg was proud of his physique and carried himself straight up, "like my favorite drink, a tall Scotch, no rocks." Only one a day, maybe half of one more near midnight," that's all."

He tried not to eavesdrop, but the barely muffled voices in the small house floated clearly and the volume rose as first Mack's, then Bobbie's urgency swelled. Reg was riveted. The recollection aroused him. His eyes squeezed shut as he leaned forward with folded arms pressing down hard on his stout knees. Mack and Bobbie were stuck. Reg expected to hear a resolution. The boy's name would reveal itself if they dug just a little bit deeper into the miasmic depths of their reluctant memories. Reggie's own silent inquiry made him sweat, and compressed tears oozed from the corners of his eyes, as he strained to both recall and forget once and for all. He felt an urge to join his friends in the inquiry, but his heart was beating fiercely and choked off his lungs. A frenzy pounded in his brain. Flashes of —————'s face, smiling, contorted in pain, laughing, pouting, cold and finally frozen like an ice sculpture, with swollen ruby lips, streamed inside his closed eyelids. A silent movie reel. He shivered and pulled the lap robe up over his head.

They had all been under suspicion. Never had so shocking and indelible an event occurred in any of their lives, and then been nearly erased from their minds. During the six week investigation, a simplistic narrative gradually blurred, came back into focus, rose to high drama, shrank to no more than three points of agreement among twelve witnesses and the principal actors: Bobbie, Mack and Reggie. A voice in Reggie's blanketed head whispered, "Jacob."

Not Adam, not Abraham. Not even close. Jacob. "Jacob", he had whispered one night in Mack's bed. Into Reginald's ear. When Jacob called him by his complete name, Reginald Scott MacDonald. When Reg heard it all together, he tingled. It felt like a secret bond. He had hidden all his life, but he knew. Rosie knew and did not mind. Reginald blushed when he felt the intermittent but familiar stirring as Jacob strode on muffled moccasin feet out of the California sun into the shadow of the swinging bar door, his hips bright in the slanted rays flickering like an early celluloid film strip across and up his golden arms. Every time, it seemed to Reg, Jacob's angel face was spotlighted for a few seconds by the two o'clock sunbeam hitting him at just the precise angle to highlight him like a key spotlight on a movie set. It crossed Reg's mind that Jacob sensed it and even paused mid-stride some afternoons, to freeze the bright pose and imprint it on viewers. On him. The leading man gilded by the cinematographer and his lighting assistant with deliberate intent. Reg relished and feared it.

Back then, Bobbie and Mack were not afraid for themselves. They worried about Reg. They weren't jealous. Reg worried about Mack. And Bobbie. He was jealous. Bobbie smiled behind those bloody lips past the clenched needle. She received enough satisfaction groping the lithe smooth quarter horse thighs and quarterback arms as she fitted and re-fitted Jacob's jeans and thread-bare shirts in regular ritualistic sessions throughout that summer of wildfire winds and soft Santana breezes that floated softly from over the low inland mountain range across the Los Angeles basin to the sea in the languid rusty Autumn. At least, that's what we all thought. At least, that's what Bobbie wanted us to think. At most, we on the outside wanted to be in on the special pleasures the Seaside Select Gang of Four—or was there a fifth?— were sharing. We were just outside, near enough and glad to be in at least the glow of their pleasures. The air, the wind, the palm fronds ripped off the tops of the coarse tree trunks, the silvery eucalyptus leaves tumbling in soft mounds around the sand-sugared feet of bronze bathers strolling to their bikes and RV's, all flashed on to Reginald Scott's mental movie screen like protective escorts of the princely Jacob in his silent stride, his woodlands honor guard. Reggie reveled in his longing, and relished every actual contact. He thought he was satisfied. But he felt used, and longed for more. We didn't know. I think now that Reggie didn't know, either.

Three closest of friends lived in separated delicate, delicious realms. Three romances, dreams, reveries. The violoncello music of longing and the swooning notes of contact were coming to a crescendo. Was it only Jacob who heard the crash of symbols and the rumble of kettle drums , felt the explosive silence that death brings? Or did the other three leave the room that night with jangled nerves, exploding fear and shredded hearts, the orchestra rearranging itself: lips, tongues and fingers, to play on without its Divo? Angel, said some. Forest music. A centaur. Swamp sprite, said some.

Some said Jacob had rounded up his family. Coven? They all showed up on time. They thought Jacob was going to announce his departure. He had made going-away noises before. He knew that made them tremble. Had anyone been in the room with him that night?

Six months after the death, the picture was swirling in all their minds and in the speculations of customers and clientele. No one said he had it in focus.

When the inquest began, many regular patrons of the bar had definite opinions, and many had only vague ideas about the four. Most I interviewed shrugged, some with wet eyes, and muttered sadly that it had seemed such a sweet setup. Bobbie and Mack and Reggie were universally respected and popular, and the newcomer who had won them over had the same effect on them and almost all their friends.

A few cried. How could this have turned so ugly? Some were frightened. I asked why. Just the air of death, and maybe murder, the feeling of being violated personally, their peaceful realm invaded by a violent act of cruelty. A personal attack. Death most foul had occurred. But not only an attack, maybe a betrayal . Of friendship? Maybe of love.

Why? Revenge? Settling of a grudge? To cover secrets? To silence a traitor? Rumors swirled about the four. Stories crept in whispers over drinks and hunched shoulders at the bar, hovered over bottles of beer in the booths. Each suspect had at least one accuser. And each inquisitor felt he knew the motive.

The truth, when it came out, shocked everyone. It surprised them, too. They were prepared, primed. But every speculation turned out to be inaccurate. You might not think so, as the time approached—it was six weeks before the inquest to began; brief, by normal standards for a suspected murder—because all the possibilities had been brought up and batted around until everyone was exhausted or just sick of the whole thing;

and almost all wished it would go away.

Someone had it right. At least one other person knew the truth. Maybe. Maybe two?

One of them? Or a stranger? 'Oh, god, no. Please don't let it be a passerby! We may never know the truth.' Could it be that even these loyal friends were wishing it turned out to be one of them, or one of the regulars at the bar, just to be relieved of the anxiety? Could it be that one or two was harboring an old grudge, some as-yet-unrevealed jealousy? They say that when trouble visits you, you find out who your real friends are. And your enemies? What about when murder comes along? Suspected murder, anyway?

The living were mourning the living. Was anyone mourning the deceased? Bobbie was. So was Mack. They were sad. This is hard for me. I'd known Mack the longest, eight years. I met Bobbie a year later, when I took a pair of torn jeans to Bobbie on Mack's recommendation. I had a bowl of her seductive stew and enjoyed an unexpected and surprisingly ribald conversation with her. She told me Eli told her two weeks before he died that he was going to the police.

"What on earth for?"

"A crime," she whispered past the needle in her mouth. "What crime?"

"He wouldn't say. At first."

"So . . . .okay . . . . what? He told you?"

"Not right away. He said, "I hope I've killed you.""

"What-the-fuck!?"

Bobbie kept sewing and snipping, straightening and ironing, an inch at a time. I waited.

"He sent me a note six months ago."

"Yeah? . . . . What did it say?" Bobbie's foot pedaled so fast that she had to pull it up to let the peddle fly and settle, so it wouldn't slam into her.

"It's in the top right kitchen drawer just past the curtain."

The note read: "Thank you. I love you. I hate you. Twelve years ago you killed my brother. One of you, anyway. But all of you together because he gave you all pleasure. He would not choose. So you loved him, and hated him. When he died, I died. But I came back. I hope I have killed you. "

I sat silent. Bobbie stopped. I swear it was the first time I'd seen her take any kind of long break from a project. I could hear the stew bubbling on the stove. Warm weary voices of beach-goers crept in under the door, cooled above by a suddenly bold August breeze entering through the screen. My heart pounded as I read, then stopped beating entirely, I would have sworn. I checked my pulse to be sure.

Bobbie spoke first. She took the letter from my lap, folded it back into the knife drawer and sat back down at the sewing machine. She resumed the hand stitching, and whispered, "I think of that note every day. I hear his voice. I almost told Mack, but he beat me to it."

"How did he ask you?"

"He didn't ask. He said he had to tell me something real bad, but was scared. Then he told me he had a note from Eli. I knew right away. He told me Eli came here to hurt us. I said "I know . . . . . now . . . . but he was always so nice. Super nice, and Mack said 'Yeah, yeah, that's it, see? Eli set us up'."

I said, "And he had a note?"

"Lord help us! He just looked at me. He looked awful. He just looked . . . . And I realized there had to be more to it."

"Sure. When did Mack say he got the note? What did it SAY?"

"Turned out about three weeks before the . . . . Eli . . . you know, jeez, maybe a couple weeks before I got mine."

"And he didn't tell you?"

"He was afraid. He thought he should shut up about it. Then he said he thought he should like, maybe warn me. But then, what would he warn me about, you know

"What did HIS NOTE SAY?"

"Same thing. I mean No, yes, I mean, same thing but more. I forgot. You know? How, when you hear something so bad, you hear it, but you don't hear it . . . or, you let it go by. Goddamn, you didn't hear what you just heard. Right? Can't be! And he said, You, too . . . you got one?"

"Yes. He said he wasn't sure I had one, and he was just shaking, you know, really shaking, he was so scared. And…"

"What? WHAT, for pity's sake?"

"He tried to figure out what Eli meant by . . . .' I hope I have killed you'."

"Oh, my God! Good Lord! You all had him, didn't you?"

Bobbie nodded. She said she told everyone, the few who asked, pried, really, that she didn't do everything anymore, and she absolutely didn't do anything all the way, not for a few years anyhow, and they believed her; but she did do him, like, almost every week. She said Eli asked for it. She serviced him. He liked that best, didn't feel like he was violating her, he told her in so many words. She liked that. It was thoughtful, like Eli. Considerate. She cried a little then, telling me she liked that best too. She thought it was less sinful . . . . and safer. Now we know that was exactly what he wanted to do, to give her, you know, the virus.

Bobbie continued: "I had to find out about Mack. I couldn't just ask him. And Reggie. I didn't know yet about Rose. It never dawned on me, I don't know now why not, but Rose? I didn't even know if they ever even met? Or where on earth they could've met to do anything. Did he hate all of us? Blame us? All of us?"

"Blame you for WHAT?" I almost screamed. It was at that moment that I realized I had to tell this story. Oh, sure, I had been writing it all along, or at least thinking it, playing scenes in my head, recalling conversations, filling in gaps of moments you don't quite recall, you know? I reconstructed some general intent, some specific assertions, and plenty of intimate details, which were vivid sometimes, and hard to actually forget. But not one of them ever described actual lovemaking or intercourse or making out. I wasn't about to ask, but like plenty of others I couldn't help wondering. We wouldn't have been far off a bunch of facts.

Adam, Abraham and Jacob, Eli. Two in four. Three in one. Four altogether? Rose never gave Reg a complete explanation. She never stopped loving him, but she knew she couldn't continue to meet with Eli and Reg together. It was Reg's idea, after Eli told him he liked Rose. Reg was excited but nervous. One day he asked her, trembling, if she would consider a threesome. She smiled, looked him in the eyes, and whispered, "Of course. " She told him later that Eli had asked her first, right after their first time in Mack's room. Reg was bewildered. Like all the rest, he believed only Eli and he knew the truth. Bella wrote scenes to the speed of her pedaling, some brief and explosive and dry ; more were slow, smooth and moist. She languished like a panting child. Mack had visions. He was a Geisha and a father, a prostitute and his own pimp, Eli his ideal client; only Eli saw it the other way around. Mack was accustomed to ruling. He had no idea that Eli ruled. Reginald Barkeep savored Eli's precious vintage. Rose was always grateful, at fifty-nine, for Eli's lust. And for the first time in her life, completely satisfied sexually.

They were all in love with love. Eli was never mechanical, never detached. But he didn't gush. Romance and seduction were his powers. And limitless versatility. If his only attraction had been beauty, his four subjects would have been merely admirers, not victims. Eli's cool passion burned away their inhibitions. Exultation overruled their guilt. And underneath it all, they truly liked him!

The inquisition, that is, the series of interrogations in the next three weeks, brought out some truths, raised new questions, and concluded little that could be called clear evidence. Many doubted there would ever be a trial. The questioning, sometimes hostile, sometimes unruly, and, when orderly, subtly accusatory, but very popular, was open to the public. The judge seemed pleased, entertained. I felt peculiar thrills emanating from him and too many in the crowds. They were delighted. Surely not with the death? With the novelty? It sickened me, but I understood. I may have been feeling a tinge of the same sophomoric thrill of the sensational. The macabre scene did not give me pleasure. With the notoriety? Too many came from outside the beach community, some from tiny, some from large suburbs as far south as San Diego and inland as far as San Bernardino. Bobbie's beach community were unhappy. Too many nearby were furious, and hostile. That made sense. But It seemed strange to me that many from outside were hostile and abusive. Fights broke out near the court house and in and near Reggie's bar. Almost all the rioters were not people who lived in or near the community.

I cannot print here the long transcripts or all the newspaper accounts, or even all my interviews with my four friends. I wish now that I had more of a foreshadowing, not of so sad and violent an ending, but at least of the dark forces that led to the event, and the opportunity to question Eli. On the few occasions we did talk, he was not shy. In fact, he seemed to enjoy our talks. He was always cordial, and, I couldn't help feeling, seductive, yes, even toward me. He couldn't help it. It was a gift. A defense, a tool, an irresistible force for survival. But a deadly charm.

At the beginning, I thought probably Mack would have answers for me, that he would be the one who knew the most. And I believed he would trust me and give me details. I was wrong. He avoided me. For the first time in our five year friendship, he clearly did not wish to deal with me. I asked him, trembling, one afternoon just as we were entering the Court, if I had upset him in some way, and he laughed. As he strode ahead into the building, he muttered, "Writers. Storytellers!" and hurried out of sight.

He was right, because here I am, trying to tell his story. Their story. Not as a hostile witness. To help them, if I could. I hadn't figured out exactly how, but I had to try to piece together some explanation that might show my friends in a good light, selfishly, to regain some peace of mind. I wasn't capable of thinking that one of them was an actual killer, so I couldn't actually think, 'Okay, so he/she couldn't stand it anymore, whatever it was—and I'll find out— exactly, and so he/she murdered him.' The complete thought was unbearable, so I could only get to 'He must've …' or 'She finally . . .' and then my mind would shut down. So what did Mack mean by "storytellers," and in that tone? Rose. She wasn't right there, so I concentrated on the other three. But one day I knew that Rose knew things the others didn't. Just like that, I knew.

I drove to Rancho Mirage. Rose looked well. She was now a redhead, which subtlety and strangely had altered her facial features. When I made that observation, she told me others had said the same thing. Then she added that the deeper truth was that she was no longer living a couple of basic emotional lies.

"You're here for the truth, aren't you?'

The coloring is meant to disguise some aging. She had a tuck of the common droopy neck, but after the hair job she was surprised as everyone else by the perplexing illusion that somehow the hair color pulled tight all the rest. When she admired the change in her mirror she would laugh, she said, and think, Must be my improved attitude. She explained that her second marriage had freed her from Reg, Mack and Bobbie, and the Danger Boys.

"You know that's why I'm here."

"You told me that on the phone."

"No, no. I was careful not to. That's interesting; I think you projected what was already on your mind… because you probably know more than I've been able to get out of all the others. The Danger Boys, wow! I'm afraid to ask, but they're the reason I came here."

"Sure."

Rose began her recollection and talked with few interruptions by me for a little over an hour. She poured us sparkling water, offered me anything else I might want, and mixed herself a medium pitcher of vodka martinis. One olive in each glassful, but a large glass bowlful next to the pitcher. I drank bottled sparkling water.

"I knew Jacob was trouble. He was also irresistible . . . . to all of us. I had him first, you know."

"Ah , , , no, I did not know. Wow."

"And I mix a better martini than Reg."

Rose was more help than I could have wished. I haven't been shocked many times in my career. I've been a writer for twenty-five years and sold my opinions as a freelance observer to legitimate, that is, honorable, publications in order to bring some clarity to hazy social events that interest simply curious regular citizens. I never thought that I was unusually naive about ordinary men and women until I ended this inquiry into this rare menage. Rose illuminated every corner of the dark realm my four friends and two catalysts inhabited over the past twelve years. I had some firm opinions at the start. By the end of my visit to Rancho Mirage, my brain was washed clean and my heart both bled and smiled.

According to Rose, the brothers were devilish angels. Complex, to be sure, but simple in their goals.

"I got out of there as soon as I figured out what Jacob was up to. I never told Reg, because I thought Jacob was enough to scare the wits out of him and Mack. I wasn't talking to Bobbie about any of it. But when Eli showed up, I knew I'd have to say something to all of them. But I chickened out at first. As long as I stayed out of town, I was okay. But whenever Reg came down to visit and Mack phoned me, I always got jittery.

So I told them what I thought of Jacob. I knew Jacob had already taken gifts and money from Reg to keep him from spreading details at the bar about his sex life. Like I said, I not only didn't mind, I was right in there with all of them. It was… stimulating.

His threats didn't frighten me, but Reg was hurt and scared. I seemed to be the only one who took Jacob at his word. Mack laughed off his pretty broad hints that he would smear him, and he didn't feel scuzzy about any of his boys. He honestly didn't care who knew. He needed to buy Jacob. It soothed his conscience. I got it.

Bobbie was the most surprising. She told Jacob nobody would believe what she was doing behind those curtains—even though she loved the idea—and she was right. Myself, I told Jacob that not one person I cared about would give a shit what he'd say about me. He was heartbroken, I swear. Not as smart as he thought. But he got darker. Meaner. He was used to getting his way. So he played a weird sad sympathy card.

He said he was depressed because he believed he was getting AIDS. Only, he never gave any proof. No tests, no symptoms, just that since we were his only sex partners, one or more of us had to be the source. I asked him if he ever said that to the others. He smiled. I didn't believe we were the only ones. What nobody could figure out was what in the hell more he wanted!. Sex, worship, kindness, a nice easy job with a few extra chores? Even respect, if you can believe it! We even talked about his honesty. Go ahead and laugh. Or sneer. What's that thing about kidnapped people falling for the kidnapper?"

"Stockholm Syndrome."

"Yeh, like that. I asked him when did he think he had AIDS. He said he wasn't sure, maybe a few months after he got here. I said, 'Then why didn't you warn us. Or, for Pete's sake, stop playing with us? He just laughed. He did blush, I'll give him that. But he smiled straight in my face and I slapped him. Hard."

"Holy crap, did he…?"

"Hit me back? Curse me? Ha! He cried. Yeah, he sobbed like a little boy, which is what he was, in a beautiful grown man's body. A scared little boy. He went down on his knees and crawled over to me. He was whimpering. He crawled up onto the couch and into my lap, with his arms around my neck. I held him in my arms. No hanky panky. We fell asleep. We woke up about a half hour later, on this couch. I was groggy, he seemed wide awake. But confused, sniveling. So, let me cut to the chase."

Rose poured herself another martini. This time I took one, too. She made it a double. I hesitated, but took it, and thanked her ahead of time for what she was about to reveal.

"Jacob killed himself."

I almost dropped my glass. I set it down, and resumed writing. I had been taking notes from the moment I had sat down.

"So did Eli."

I put up my hand, put down the notepad and pen, lay back in the armchair and closed my eyes. Rose was silent. After fifteen minutes or so, I opened my eyes. Rose had not changed her position, still leaning forward with both elbows on her knees, hands clasped, holding the stem of the martini.

"He had fallen in love. I asked with which one. Not with me? He laughed a little. He said he had been rejected. But he kept seeing all of us. He begged the one he wanted. He was told to just leave. He told me that Jacob had the same experience with one of us. Good Lord, can you believe us?!

He said when Jacob had finally been able to break away and come home, to him, Jacob told him the story, even though Eli was only a child.

Their Mum—he called her— had just passed away—and Eli was his only kin. Two years later, when Eli was twelve, Jacob came back. It was as if he had never left. Everyone celebrated, and the gang was all here. We partied every week, one after another. The sex was the best any of us ever had. We didn't say much out of school, and some nights, or on stormy afternoons when the bar was closed for a few hours, we met all together. Yeah. Disgraceful! In that back room. There was a lot of switching around. I won't shock you with details."

"I'd love to hear."

"I'm sure. But not this time.

"Raincheck? Forgive the pun."

"Sure."

"The night Jacob passed, we had all gone to the room for a helluva heavenly orgy, we thought. The room was dark. Mack flipped the switch. No lights. He called Jacob's name. The moon was a wide shaft through the high window down to the corner near the closet. The rest is still a nightmare. It's like an old old movie in my brain. In my heart. It was so real, so harsh, real black and white in that dark shadowy room. There were glasses and all our favorite drinks. A pitcher of martinis like mine, diet sodas, cans of seltzer. Never thought it was a setup. We were all horny. It was the most erotic atmosphere I'd ever been in.

We stayed about an hour. Jacob was tipsy, but not drunk. He performed a dance while stripping down to a yellow g-string. He was raging. We were going nuts. Quietly. I think Reg and I got into it and I kind of woke out of a swoon or something feeling Mack on me. Bobbie was servicing him. Mack was all over me with his hands and mouth, then all over Reg. We were all drunk, but not on booze. The moon was down around midnight, so the room was darker than usual. Every one of us had been there in the darkest nights some time or other. We were used to fumbling, We moaned and groaned a lot, but nobody talked. Around one A.M. I got up to leave. I bumped into Bobbie at the door. She laughed. I kissed her on the mouth. We left. Mack and Reg and Jacob were still inside, because I looked back from the end of the alley to see if anyone was following. I never found out what happened after we left. Bobbie told me later that Mack stumbled in

116

around 2:00 and passed out on her couch."

The next day all hell broke out. Phone calls, cops, people coming around screaming and talking a hundred miles an hour. Questions, swearing, crying. Jacob was dead. They found him fully clothed slumped on the bathroom floor. There was vomit. His forehead was bleeding, probably from hitting the sink, first; there was blood in the basin, then maybe hitting it again on the edge of the toilet. No sign of violence. They said he looked normal, even peaceful. I went nuts. It took me days to stop crying. Reg was so sweet. Mack and Bobbie, too. Mack was just so sad. He helped, though. We got food together. Nobody said much. "

"What about the police?"

"Oh, god! They were very polite. But they were pissed off, I think."

"Why?"

Well, they had a corpse, they had glasses and bottles and fingerprints and lots of saliva and even sperm samples. Disgusting, right? But no wild messed up bed or clothes thrown around, no blood except Jacob's. And no bruises on him. They stripped all of us within two days. Looking for scratches or bruises on us. We were very orderly. Ha! Messed up lives, but organized! Orgy-anized I used to say. Bad joke. Jacob wanted evidence left. He thought we would be blamed and somehow convicted.

'All of you?! Pretty vicious. '

"Yeah, I know. Good Lord! Did he hate us that much? But you know, we didn't hate him, even then. We were all depressed."

"What did the cops do?"

"It didn't take long for public defenders to get appointed. When they told us we all needed lawyers, we said no. We told them everything."

"Everything?

"Every little detail. And boy, did they lap it up! I'm sure they expected us to rat on each other, or each to make excuses to save his own ass, or maybe just come clean and tell them we took advantage of the gorgeous dumb fuck and decided to cover up the "scandal" by ganging up and getting rid of him. I said to the guy who acted like the most professional guy they gave us—there were only three—did he think we would have been so sloppy as to leave obvious evidence behind? He was pretty hip. He wanted to laugh, I could tell, but he was a gent, I have to say. He just smiled a little and shook his head."

"Okay! So . . . what did Jacob die of?"

"God in heaven, I think he made a terrible mistake. I'll never know exactly why he turned on us. He must've built up some crazy scenario about us scheming all together to use him and then maybe got scared that we'd just throw him away once we were satisfied. His mother had left when he and his little brother were little, and his pa had molested him and then run off with, are you ready ... the local minister! He did say he was in love with one us, to Bobbie once, twice to me, and I'd guess to Mack and Reg. You know, I love him no matter what, but I think if Reg could've let himself open up completely, he and Jacob could've maybe been together. Both would have been relieved."

"So, what happened?"

"Jacob took pills just after we left. He thought they would blame us. Or at least one of us, though I couldn't see how they could've singled out anybody. One person. Could be he actually believed we could all get the blame. Just ornery. Confused, yeah. But I figure he got just enough sense at the last second to know it was nuts, and tried to come out of it. But it was too late. So, he got us accused, alright. And hassled. And gave us a lot of pain. Punishment, I guess he called it, for not loving him or wanting him enough. His way. All the way, whatever that was. He must've passed out. When he came to, he panicked, because we were gone, but also because he didn't want to die, so he tried to throw up. His cell phone was open, just under the bed. He probably tried to call 911, but lost control. Then he tried to drink all the booze he could, to help him throw up. You know, he was practically allergic to alcohol, said when he was a little boy they made him drink that rot gut they brew down there in the swamp. Damn, he must have suffered so at that moment! Trying to stop what he'd started. Horrible!"

Rose was weeping. She was quiet for a long time. We kind of napped, I think. I mean, I closed my eyes. She was curled up on the couch. We were both beaten up by our feelings, by the overall tension. By saying the words out loud. What a hell it must've been for them for such a long time. For the first time, my heart went out to Reg. And to Mack. I never dreamed I'd feel so much sympathy for him. He was sensitive, okay, and a good friend to me, but always steady, put together. I never thought of him as penetrable, I mean, seriously vulnerable. But the picture was clearing up for me. I guess I had been feeling awkward about imagining certain intimacies, their getting together, what they did with each other. Hard to let myself concentrate on details. Now I felt their pain.

After maybe, like, fifteen minutes, Rose was whimpering. Then she sat up and continued.

"They found thrown up booze and vomit near the bed and on the phone, in and around the toilet. One woman officer said he looked like a peaceful angel when they cleaned him up and put him on the stretcher."

"So you were all let go?"

"Not right away. For weeks they went over and over the evidence. One of the attorneys, the youngest one, got it better than the rest. He was maybe thirty-five, cute. Smart. He had seen a lot of television. He wrapped it all up for me one afternoon. I almost made a pass at him. Well, maybe I did, only he laughed and let it slide before I embarrassed myself. We let the whole thing slide, too. But it never went all the way away. Still. Then when Eli showed up, Lord! Twelve years in between. You'd think at least one of us would have had some kind of deja due or a hunch or a little bit of awareness to sense something odd. Weird. As weird as the first go-round? Ha! Weirder."

"Okay. So, the verdict?"

"They had a lot of evidence that there was a party, and we were all there. They tried their damnedest to nail someone. But there was actually too much to go on, too much to separate. They were stumped. They couldn't get enough evidence to throw at any one of us. They tried to apply RICO, you know, that gang stuff?"

"Sure, a collusion, one maybe the ringleader but all guilty of the same intent, to get rid of him. "

"But they couldn't figure why. No real motive, since we all got what we wanted. They never figured it was Jacob who wasn't satisfied with what he got, or didn't get."

"I stood up, signaled that I need the toilet, and she pointed to over my shoulder. When I came back, she had wiped away her tears and some streaky makeup, and had a new martini resting in her hand on both knees.."

"As I sat back down," she said"

"Oh, but they had a very short note. Printed in pencil. It says, 'They killed me.'"

"Crap! And even that didn't . . . . . wait, you just said 'it says.'. They have it?"

"No, I have it."

Months later, after the verdict and some paper work, they believed me when I told them his family wanted me to get it and send it to them. I asked them why they didn't talk to the parents themselves. You know what that tough D.A. said? He said they felt sorry for the boy. Apart from the first initial contacts with the family, they didn't want o face the mom and dad. And one of them told me they felt even sorrier for us. Go figure."

"So, now they have to be thinking these people are diabolical or nuts or just stupid. I mean, to do something, or be involved in something so close to the first time, they just gotta be guilty of SOMETHING."

"They had no case. I'm sure some of the cops are still wondering. Some are saying I told you so, after this, now. I don't know when I'll go back. Maybe never. Say Hi to Reg. Tell Mack and Bobbie I'm here … if they want…"

"Sure."

"I kissed her on the forehead and both cheeks, hugged her hard, and let myself out."

Not credible. No. No way. For six more months witnesses were brought in for questioning. Regulars from the bar. People who used the back alley to sneak out of the bar, or to get to their cars parked near the beach. A drunk who was found hours after the police had conducted what they thought was a thorough search. He had been drinking his last pint of rye when all the sirens were screeching and feet had been slipping past on the cobblestones while auto tires were bouncing on the uneven surface, when the lights of the cop cars and the ambulance were sending sharp streaks of blood red and yellow into the folds of his concealing blanket behind the dumpsters where he cowered.

The four were questioned until the cops and the D.A. and they, too, were numb. Worn out. Nothing new came out. Except the autopsy report. Eli had suffered a sudden and severe heart attack!

The summation? He had set them up. He thought the notes might bring them around to regarding him more seriously. More than a dalliance. He wanted to put the fear of the Devil himself in each one, as he would have put it. He wanted them to feel sorry for him, for one in particular to confess true love and take him in forever, instead of using and rejecting him as they did Jacob. He never specified which one. He had AIDS, all right, but the report concluded "undetectable," So there was little chance that he would have infected anyone. And if his own fear had not prevented him from getting a medical opinion, he likely would have had years to live. So sad. But, perhaps the heart attack was lurking all along. Bobbie wanted to believe that. Mack hoped so, too. It felt less painful to accept than the grim reality of Eli's scheme and the sordid details and circumstances of the staged frame up and Eli's vicious vengeful intent. I was reminded of William Saroyan's refrain in "The Time of Your Life.": 'No foundation. All the way down the line.'

The speculation did not stop. The verdict was accidental death. The version the police published and the one everyone of us but Reg subscribes to is this: When everyone left, Eli was in the bathroom. Somehow, they all noticed at once, and something told them to just get out. When Eli emerged, he must've been upset. When they found him, the room had been torn up, almost every object broken or torn, glass shards everywhere. Eli was naked and bleeding. The rope was around his neck. There were marks on the bathroom door that looked as if made by a rope rubbing over the top edge, the wastebasket was overturned, and the top hinge of the door was loose, so the door had slipped partially off the frame when Eli tried to slam it behind the big knot on the short noose. Eli was only about five feet six, like Alan Ladd, his favorite movie star, he had told everybody.

He was drunk, no question, and he tried to hang himself. But it all fell apart. He probably passed out, came to, drank some more and staggered over to the bed. His face was streaked with tears and blood, and his feet were cut the coroner reported. He my have passed out. Everyone hoped he was unconscious when his heart stopped.

Things fade, even seemingly indelible tragedies, but ballads don't. They are sung for as long as a single note, or at least a memorable bar or two are playing in someone's head.

The Meeting

He walked down the four steps, turned right and hurried along the sidewalk for a dozen yards, noting the Great Dane standing on the subterranean concrete outside the window of the basement apartment. After he passed the fourth house, he slowed his pace and smiled, swung one leg out jerkily at the roadway and grunted with a laugh: "Hnng, uhhh, hee!"

Never mind, he thought. I'll be there and no one will be able to deny me. His thoughts tiptoed, but hard, on point. Tradition, he had decided, is a way of falsifying life. It is a grand orderly lie that gives substance to flimsy everyday doings. Well, he would play the game even better, now that he had found something worth choosing.

Luce was different. She didn't think at all like him, and if he ever explained one of his profundities to her, she would laugh, he knew. Luce would not laugh, but she didn't think it was her place to tell that to Schlomo, even if she wanted to hear his latest thought. She heard plenty, though, of what he said to others, so she didn't feel left out. That was one of Scuro's methods, probably, to make sure he talked in detail to his friends when Luce was near.

His friends wondered why he was quiet when they were alone with him and not only talkative but loud whenever Luce showed up, because often after Luce had left he would say, "Geez, I hope she doesn't go tell everybody that stuff."

Schlomo reached the corner, sped up the side stairs, shouldered open the swing door, lurched to the nearest chair, and sat. "Hi, silly."

"Huh?"

"You saw me."

"I knew you were coming."

"You saw me."

"Half a block away, thinking. Sweating. What's going on in there?"

"I can't see you now."

"Open your eyes."

"I'm looking."

"Good. Come on, what're you scheming? All those thoughts skittering around in there. Teeming brain." She twirled both forefingers around his temples and pinched one of his cheeks. "Nice face, though. Handsome. Simple . . . but handsome."

"I got a plan. I'm gonna tell it to Tove, see if he thinks it'll work."

"Tell it to me." Sometimes thoughts clustered up in her brain like tittering children in a cloakroom. She despaired of ever working one clear, separate, sensible, on those occasions. Oh, well, feelings mattered more, anyway, everyone knew that, and being nice, doing nice things for people and maybe looking pretty or at least tidy, with a little bit of fun, you know, flair or what is that, what you call it? Oh, yeah, style. I've got style. My own. Don't know exactly what it is, but I can feel it.

Schlomo was just on the other side of the door, talking it over with the rest of the gang, well . . . the Club. They called it the Club, but other people, especially when they saw the band swarming down the streets like a school of sharks or loping single file like one of those long dragon kites, whispered and worried and called the children "the bunch." That bunch of boys and that girl, who should know better. The trouble that bunch was going to make!

"They made a lot of trouble already, huh?" It was the Man. He had been around for a couple of weeks, most people said, but Schlomo said at the hardware store that he'd been living in the back of the school annex for over a month. Schlomo knew because the Man had come in to buy a kerosene lantern then, only he said right up front that he couldn't exactly pay for it, but he would work for it or run errands, maybe, or make deliveries, perhaps. The Man said "perhaps" instead of maybe. The Man said "I'm gratified." Schlomo was tickled by those words; they sounded grand compared to "maybe:" and "grateful." He thought the Man was genteel. But the other people in the town thought the man was spooky, and they worried about the trouble he was going to make. The Man walked for hours every day, in and out of stores and restaurants up and down Main Street, even sitting for up to a half hour with the firemen and with policemen at the station. After his first week in the town, Schlomo began following him. On every visit the Man asked carefully if he could talk to the detainees in the three cells. Schlomo noted that the Man never called them prisoners They never sassed him; they listened to his words of comfort.

People had their minds made up. "No, they ain't made any trouble yet, but they're bound to. I mean, what do they think, they can jus' go around like that?"

"Go around like what?" said the Man.

"Well, they gang up, like, an' go behind the Elks Club in that little park, and sometimes they even get in the building, in the lobby, like, right there in the front."

"What do they do there?"

"Come on! You know . . . they make . . . plans. They scheme and plot and sneak around, decidin' what kinda trouble to get in next."

"What trouble have they made so far?"

"Aw, shut up! I don't wanna talk to you . . . anyway . . . what you know about it, huh?"

The Man said, "I'm trying to find out, although it's none of my business, you're right. I should shut up about it."

Schlomo had to tell or burst. Scuro would listen this time. So why didn't he tell Scuro his plan? He would. Straight through the door and right out of his mouth and quick as that, the decision would come. And Schlomo would be Scuro's lieutenant and they would all respect their new leader. A new tradition could begin. A new dynasty. Pure and grand, but not impossible. He was a practical dreamer.

"Traditionally," he intoned too dramatically, "we have been held . . uh, thought of . . . as ruffians, you know, rowdies." The boys glared at him for the most part. Kiku was smiling, though. He was half hidden from all the rest including Scuro, with only one of his eyes showing from over Schlomo's left shoulder. Scuro liked Schlomo's flair: "Guts is what he's got."

"But we're hard workers," Schlomo continued, a little less grandly, "and we need a place to work, a center of operations, and then a project we can all participate in which could get us enough money to pay our way."

"Yeah, we gotta make some dough."

"Right on, okay."

"Let's hear it!"

The stranger was amused. He liked the formal, stiff stern language of the meeting. It sounded like children in a play. Preparing to change the world. A League of Nations. A Supreme Court. The Children's Crusade.

"What about him?" A finger on a long high arm pointed to the stranger in the back.

Half a dozen voices, almost in unison: "Who cares? He don't know. . . . . He's okay . . . he don't even live here."

"What if he's a spy?"

"You wanna ask him?"

"What? He wouldn't tell . . . if he was. But what if he was? Is?!"

"I think he can hear you. Go ahead, ask him."

Someone else shouted out the question: "Hey, Stranger, are you a spy?"

"Yes."

Schlomo shouted, "Shit! Okay, who you spying for?"

"Me. Is that okay? I won't tell anybody but myself. And maybe later I can help."

Schlomo raised his voice for all to hear: "Anybody care anymore?"

The room shouted "No!"

Another voice shouted "Just keep going."

Schlomo resumed.

The meeting went on for three days. Most of the boys never left the basement. Some went home on short relief runs, for food they missed or clean underwear or just for the sense of adventure that they were away on a terrible mission, forced to be separated from safe homes, to sacrifice comfort, perhaps never to return to refrigerators and television sets and beds and private toilets, because this assignment meant everything, even though families back there might never understand the price and the weight of these proceedings and the urgency that propelled these pioneers toward a new beginning.

This would be a new alliance of strength, bound by thoughts not new but newly, uniquely combined, to produce a sweet Gargantua of philanthropy, patriotism, camaraderie and joy, a beneficent Monster which would prowl the prairies (out in Nebraska?), the streets and alleyways, the highways, hills, hollows (Kentucky, right?), mountains, even, but especially back rooms and upstairs rooms, and under the eaves way, way up there where some of the weirdest but most available creatures snuggled or cowered. Available in the sense of susceptible, eager, as the emancipators were, to escape and expand and maraud, but merrily, the land masses and the masses living in the lands of faraway and here, near, next door, down the road, right at the kitchen table, under the table, in basements, in the sewers; to tell them the good news and hug them into joining the search for more out of life so that all together they could, once and for all, at long last—too, too long—change things.

"To what?"

"Oh, man! It's him again. Butt out, will ya?" The Man smiled, held up both hands, palms forward with widely spread uncommonly long fingers, and eased backwards to press himself against the rear wall.

"Anyone who's here is with us, I figure. Those other people don't even ever come near us. What ya think, this guy is some kind of spy? He don't even come from around here."

Many present were confused now. What Schlomo and the objector were talking about, they alone took for granted. No, Luce understood, too. She was standing so close to the Stranger that her right hand brushed his. She felt a spark. Static electricity, maybe, or maybe something better. She glowed, or maybe she was shining with pride in Schlomo's confidence or his defense of an innocent visitor, or just with the excitement filling the room, and maybe the spark had shot the other way, from her to the Stranger.

His thick hair was wavy and white and neat. His skin was parchment, golden and tight and patterned, but not with wrinkles, like a translucent map or a lampshade with the light on inside. His big hands hung suspended on thick thumbs from his belt, his head bowed. Smiling every time he looked up, he showed only upper teeth, pure white and even. Luce stared and thought she should look away, but the man didn't notice this time.

He smiled at the boys up front, sometimes in a half yawn, as if about to ask a question. Schlomo didn't like the interruption, which it was, because every time he thought the man was going to speak, he hesitated. That made him sound uncertain, as if he had a stutter. Schlomo pressed on.

"We are gonna improve things. But first we have to get rid of tradition, or change it. We have got to turn it around, ya know? It's tradition to buy as much as you want of certain stuff and throw it away when it's sort of used and then buy some more. It's a tradition to have twelve different kinds of toilet paper, you know, colors and patterns and this many sheets per roll and that many square inches or feet and even perfume, or whatever. It's a tradition to sell things pretending, pretending that this does such and such, but it doesn't! But never mind, because we just want to sell it, right, so what if it doesn't really do it, that's their problem, okay? They can just buy some other thing. It's a tradition to chemicalize everything, to color it and colorize it and salt it and sugar it and preserve it and glutamate it and radiate it and crisp it and wax it and hormone it and oil and butter it and over-cheese it inside the crust!"

The man looked for Schlomo's notes, but Schlomo was speaking A

Capella, no sheet music. He wondered how this young man could be so aware. Luce had never heard any of this from Schlomo.

Inside the hardware store, Beal, Hazel, and Mocassin were bickering: "Hazel, your boy is one of 'em," said Beal. Beal was Mocassin's oldest friend, from grade school. He and Moc and Pal all loved Hazel. But not all at once. Moc carried her books in the fifth grade. Beal had taken her to the prom in high school. Pal drove her around in his dad's convertible, and married her. After he was gone six years, Hazel agreed to marry Moc, even though they weren't at all sure Pal was dead or just gone forever.

"That don't make him bad, Moc. I get so mad anymore because I can't do even one woman's hair without hearing about what bad stuff those kids is up to. I raised him alone, but he's okay. He don't sass me. He won't use his daddy's name, but he don't say he misses 'm or is mad at the world because he left," said Hazel.

Moc said, "Yeah? Well maybe he still does . . . . and is, but just won't say so."

Beal said, "Schlomo idolizes him."

Hazel sneered. "Yah, sure, figures. He never knew him, but he's his hero."

"Hey, Beal, I thought you didn't go with hero worship. You never would say that before," said Moc. And by the fucking way, you know he's Samuel! What the fuck?! You never called him Schlomo before. Or am I forgetting things?

"Maybe I changed my mind."

"Maybe you don't have a mind to change," said Moc.

"Well, what got you so hot so sudden? Maybe you ARE forgetting things , like I'm still your best friend—well, one of two of 'em, anyway, I thought," said Beal.

"Cuz I don't think it's so great that a man gets to run off and nobody, nobody criticizes it! I gotta do my job and stay put and walk the line, and some weirdos can jus' stroll away an' screw cheerleaders and other men's wives, maybe, for all I know."

"Well, you not only don't know it all, you don't know shit! I mean, what's that got to do with Schlomo, I mean Sam, fer Christ sake, SIR?! AND top of everything ELSE, you get to have Hazel because Pal left! So, what the fuck you griping about?

"Geez, I know who the weirdo is. Geez," said Moc

"Mocassin, you got a lot of poison in you, you really do. Boy, I knew you were mad about something in particular, like for months, but you been deeply upset for a great long time, I see that," said Hazel.

"So?"

"So, you would do better not to take it out on your friends, never mind ME."

"Hazel, the truth is, I don't regard anyone here as a real friend." The room was too quiet. "I don't, I'm sorry. No, I take it back. I ain't sorry. Not a bit! I'm not."

It was Mocassin who was squirming, not the others. They just couldn't look at him. He thought to apologize to Hazel, at least, but every sentence that came into his head seared his tongue. Beal touched Moc's shoulder and spoke without looking at him.

"I don't have a son, like you, Moc. . . . Hazel, so I can't act like I know how that feels, exactly, but I think I seen how you both have a lot of anxiety and hurt about these young fellows. But I never see you telling them. 'Course, I don't know any what goes on behind closed doors, but I see them boys around, too, and they never seem to talk about it, and I never hear that they do. I never heard Samuel complain. I hear a lot, though, the two of you beating up on other folks with no cause. It's not fair."

Hazel said, "Shit, Moc, see, there you go again, always like that. It's never you." She had slept with all three of them half a dozen times each before she settled on Pal. "You all can't think about anything but yourself, that's all, that's why yer all mad still. And you are all jealous, jay-ee-ell-you-ess, ess, ess. Definitely, for sure!" Hazel waited for a response.

She flipped, with vigor but no apparent purpose, through the rack of cards on the revolving carousel. Hazel knew she'd wounded them, and sort of regretted it. But she'd "had to use a shotgun to get one rat", she told herself, and couldn't help bloodying some less fang-toothed types. She knew they all carried vermin. Some of them, poison. And she included herself. The ache that made her strike now was too much to contain today. Today she knew that when Pal left, her breath went out the door with him.

He was backwards-and-forwards, all right. That's how he got the nickname: Palindrome. One day their English teacher gave the class "A man, a plan, a canal, Panama!" Beal laughed and said, "Whooah, yeah, that's you, good buddy, backwards-and-forwards . . . and back again. You're a palindrome, all right. Pal." And it stuck. He said it so much that it irritated people. He was already "King Arthur Bogus." Hazel thought that was pretty high already, and why would he want just plain "Pal?" Just a friend, a bud, a little thing. Not like King or Buck or Rocky, a big man's title. Arthur wanted people to think of him as a buddy, to like him like that. To be popular. Not that he was ever going to be your real friend, no way, didn't they wish, a lot of these people. Then he ran away.

Moccasin sat down and began rocking, even though the chair wasn't exactly a rocker. It had turned into one from so much tilting back and forth, like what he was doing now, so that the legs were uneven and let you roll a little. Rocking and rolling, he looked only at the floor. He looked back at Hazel, really angry.

"Well, someone's alive and has his hearing. What are you looking at? Me? Or yourself, or . . . who . . . <u>whom</u>?"

Beal stood next to Hazel, checking out the small hand tools next to the card rack. He didn't want to give the wrong idea that he needed to side with anyone, especially not Hazel. Suddenly, he rose and walked up to her. He held her too tight by both arms. Hazel wasn't sure if she was going to get clobbered, even though she couldn't imagine Beal slugging anyone, least of all a woman. He held her hard and stared into her face. Hazel stared back.

"Good!" and he laughed. He kept on laughing until Hazel smiled. Then he walked back behind the counter and waved toward the door, as he checked the pot of coffee at the far end. He flipped over the OPEN sign and pulled down the shade and stood facing the blank parchment. Hazel stopped spinning the cards and looked at Beal. Mocassin finished rocking on a forward tilt and kept his gaze on the floor.

Mocassin said, "Nobody ever seen this fella before . . . so is anyone thinking what I'm thinking? Is that why maybe yer so worried, Liz, and so mad? "Beal didn't understand. Hazel needed an arm, so she took Beal's and put her head on his shoulder for a moment, then let go altogether. Beal was embarrassed.

At the meeting, the Stranger raised his hand. Sort of. He didn't even bring it all the way up, but the silence was quick.. Had every single one of them been watching him, or did he have a power? 'How on earth did he do that?' Luce wondered. No one looked at him directly, except for Schlomo, who ran right over. They smiled at each other and the Stranger asked, "How you gonna get'em to give up their most prized possession?"

"What's that?", asked Luce.

"Their rage, Luce." And the Stranger flashed down a smile that seemed to illuminate her face. She beamed back her surprise.

Before he realized it, Schlomo had murmured, 'Right on.' Luce was pleased but surprised again. The Man began to move, and the sharks made way. He could have been Noah in the depths, or Ahab on the prow, but he was no avenger.

A few passersby stood outside discussing the early closing. Some shook the doorknob, staring straight at the CLOSED sign. Hazel went on, "I don't know if he's back, but his kind of thinking sure is."

"What do you mean by that . . . what?!" said Moccasin.

"Oh, relax, I don't mean you or anybody here." She saw the looks from all of them that said, 'I don't think that way. I don't cheat or run off or break peoples's hearts, or lie or just do as I please, no. No sir.'

Hazel was tickled.

How had she stayed, breathing this stale air, rubbing her hands up and down raised arms subconsciously wiping off the dingy mist that coated her skin.

"He might come back. No, fuck him and his "higher pursuits! Above all of them, the world, humankind? What kind did he think he was? Non-human? Sub-human? Probably super-human. if you ask me. He was going out to fix things. Like what things, I must've asked him a million times."

She had needed to love him. She had needed to stop loving him. She had needed to forget. She had needed to hold the love, even if it was only with her one-sided grip. She needed him back. She had to stay, because it could happen, but only here. She could never have tracked him down. He had to return. He was Pal. Forward and backward. In and out. Away and back. She was one way only. Here. Now. Herself. But not. His.

The Man was leaving.

Hazel went behind the counter and leaned over near the cash register, with her arms wrapped over her ample bosom, hands clasping her bare shoulders, and her chin thrust down not quite far enough to touch the pink bulges above her bra. It was a familiar position. It usually signaled a serious statement. She waited until everyone saw it, dropped her eyes, sighed and whispered, almost too quietly but with emphasis for even the nearest listener to hear, "Okay! I know what you all are thinking, and you're right. That is, you don't know the details, but you know the gist, the thrust, the fucking foundation on top of which all our fights and petty bullshit have been fought and keeps being crapped down on everybody and on this gouged out, slimy floor. It's a repository, this store and this floor, and our filthy heads, for our crapped out dreams and resentments. I'm gonna give you all a break. And I'm already wondering what the fuck will happen next, when I'm through, even though I do't have a habit of getting too far ahead of myself. Don't worry, I'll be quick. . . . . . . for me.

When I agreed to marry Pal, "Arthur Bogus," nothing but a lowdown Hillbilly, like all of us, he gave me a command. Not a request. Not even a take-it-or-leave it thing! "King" Bogus made me promise, as if I hadn't been doing it right along already, to sleep with you, Beal, and you, Moc, not just a couple of times each, but over and over each, and of course with him, until he was ready to marry me. I was stumped for words. Me, the fastest mouth in the county! Yeah, go ahead and laugh, if yer not too stunned or too embarrassed to admit you knew all along, but didn't care. But I'll bet you didn't know why Pal wanted that, huh? Because the son-of-a-bitch did not want to be sure when I got pregnant whose kid it was gonna be. Every father on earth is damned just-about-insane about knowing the truth of whether he is the father of the child whenever that's a question for all kinds of fucking reasons you hear about, but not the "King!" He wasn't gonna be tied down by THAT little detail. Cold, right? Hard, you think? Mean, really really mean! Right?

But it's worse. I was worse. He added, about a week after, when I'd gone all the way with you, Moc, and you, Beal, maybe twice each, I don't exactly remember. Because I was having a good time. Pal would ask me to describe each "session," he called them. One time he laughed and said, "Ha! You are having the time of your life. You thought I was horrid and crazy, but you like this." He was right. He made me so mad that I told him I was expanding my horizons, because HE liked it so much. This time, King Arthur shut his mouth, the second fastest in the county.

The gimpy chair was still, stuck to the floor by Beal's slumped body. His hands were in his lap, clasped tight, his chin was on his chest, his legs stretched full out resting on crossed feet, eyes staring into space. Mocs eyes were closed. He stood upright leaning against the counter, next door to the cash register. You'd expect him to fall over, he was so rigid , which made him look extra tall. He was already six two. His thumping heart signaled distress through his trademark plaid shirt which was stretched tight because his hands were clasped up behind his neck, maybe holding him from falling straight backwards, maybe so they wouldn't fly to Hazel's throat, where his brain was likely willing them.

Had they known all along? Did Hazel want them to know? Did she play one off the other and both off Pal? Was Pal the puppeteer, or was Hazel?

Hazel was shutting down. For twelve years Hazel took out her scorn for Pal on Moc and Beal. She sneered at Beal's girlfriends. He'd bring them around sometimes just to rouse her interest. Every one was younger, and most people would agree that they were prettier. None, however, could match Hazel's intelligence or wit or energy. Her skin was smooth; she warned both men and women not to go sun-burning. She ate no meat, didn't smoke after age twenty-three, even though she'd started on her father's non-filter extra long Pall Malls when she was fourteen. And her shape was a product of the Jane Fonda workout videos. She never competed. She waited. Beal had maybe two dozen high school cheer leaders and half of their moms in those twelve years. He was a fit ex-jock who kept his looks after high school, played quarterback a year in college, dropped out and worked construction for his dad's carpentry firm, lost almost no hair on the top of his head, shaved his chest and even his pubes, was naturally smooth under his arms, and had so light a natural beard that even at thirty-nine he shaved only every other day. He was a ginger. Hazel never let on that his skin and curly red hair, lightly freckled back and arms and thighs gave her hot flashes almost every day that she saw him.

Beal had quick orgasms. His girls took that to mean that he was sexually robust, and each one just knew she excited him most. The opposite was true. Beal had raging erections he could never sustain. Two minutes tops, and he'd spray all over the place. He was never going to be a father. And he was never going to have what almost any man would call sexual satisfaction. He had sexual relief. Often. But even though he'd swear if pressed under oath to confess, he'd never admit that he was anything but a bona fide virile stud who couldn't get enough sexual satisfaction, he was seldom satisfied. It took him over ten years to realize that his love for Hazel was never going to be returned, and his frantic lust required from her alone some sure evidence of what he'd read, though seldom heard described by anyone he knew, as "true love."

Moc was a different case. He never loved Hazel, and sex with her was therapeutic, though he would never have thought or put it that way. Not just relief, his long sessions of foreplay, with giggles and playful pain, pleased both of them. Their secret. Moc wondered what secrets Beal and Hazel shared. All three were clean freaks. Hazel said so, to her best friend.

"I couldn't stand Pal's dirty fingernails. He was so pure about everything else. He never had a pimple. No bunions. He said my feet were pretty. You know what? His were, too. Honest. Kinky, huh? No, I mean, honest, he was perfect. Perfect teeth, perfect hair, perfect skin. He had nice ears. It wasn't all put together like a movie star or something, he wasn't pretty, you know, but handsome. With a pretty mouth, though. That mouth. That's what I wanted a baby for, from him. Pal's mouth. Sound weird? Yeah, maybe, but I dreamed about his mouth. I imagined his baby and nursing that little thing with Beal's mouth. Boy or girl, oh, all right, maybe I wished sort of more for a boy doing that on me, my boy. Pal's boy. But nah, a girl would be okay, too. A tiny girl with Pal's mouth sucking on my nipple. Pal did that to me. On me. I never told that to anyone, ever, ever. Never told Pal. But he told me stuff. Too much. But not his secrets.

I thought all his stories about all his girls, women, both, all ages, were secrets he was sharing. But no. After he left, they came around. One by one by one. The girl at the dry cleaners. The China doll girl.. And she was. I mean, looked just like a doll, not a human girl.. Clean! Whew, squeaky clean. I thought, Yeah, Pal wants clean. I was, really, but not as pretty.

She would deliver my waitress dresses. I'd say, You don't have to do that. She'd say, I know, but kept doing it. I tried to tip her. She said, No, I deserved it because I worked so hard. How sweet, I thought. Then I got it. She was looking for Pal. Even after we all knew he was gone they would come around, just to, like, hope he might come back, or something, or just to be where he used to be, you know, and what, I don't know, feel him here? like he wasn't actually gone gone, forever or something?

Funny. That China doll upset me. But I felt better, because I had his baby and she didn't. Or, I didn't know for sure. Maybe she had one, too. I never saw any. Aw, shit!

What if I see a little boy with Pal's face and with clean fingernails and slanted, you know, eyes, coming in here. And that mouth. No, I didn't want to see that."

"Did you tell Pal your secrets? Or didn't . . . don't you have any? Aw, shit, everyone has . . . some. So, did you?"

"I have the biggest one. I'm a liar. And a cheat."

Moc and Beal were statues. As if they had mocked the gods or forgotten that they rule. If you broke their rules too many times, they put you down. Or tore you up. Or just left you all alone to break yourself.

And if you looked Medusa in the eyes, you could turn to stone. Hazel felt her power. She had always been brighter and quicker. She didn't run her business into the ground the way the men did. Every one. They all ended up needing her. And she had always needed them to depend on her. Venus? Medusa. Until Pal. She thought she had the sure thing until she took his order to lay herself out to all three, so Pal wouldn't feel trapped. But from that moment fourteen years ago, she tied a knot around her heart Her eyes watered, and she bled invisible blood. Blood of remorse, of longing and of hatred. She admitted to herself that she wanted all three men. But she took precautions. Except with Pal. His was the only child she craved. She couldn't hold him, but the child could. He was afraid of that, so he made her promise. Pal told her he was leaving to find himself.

"I used to tell him I knew who he was. I could tell him, if he asked. He would laugh. I would say, 'Maybe a son could help you find yourself'

Do you two remember anything at all about the weeks just before Pal left? Probably not. Okay, remember how many times you, Moc, begged me to let you come over? How many times I said No when you said all you wanted was to hold me tight, naked, not asking for anything more, just so you could feel I didn't hate you or anything, so you could sleep, because you hardly could, you were so afraid I was off you entirely? And you, Beal, even though you had all those girls, telling me they couldn't satisfy you like I could? . . . . I didn't sleep with either one of you for five months and six days, exactly. I got pregnant, but only saw Pal.

I made sure the only possible seed growing in my belly was Pal's. I missed you both, I admit it. But I told Pal I was having a hot time. I made it sound like he was giving me permission, hell, a goddamn ORDER to run wild and feel good about it. Fooled THAT poor sonofabitch! He would laugh, and asked if he was still my favorite lover He said right off that he was set to go. He said it so many times, that I knew I couldn't believe him. I was scared each time. But he stayed. He thought if he said it over and over he could confuse me. and I would keep being with Moc and Beal and probably others, he'd make sure that he wasn't the father. Dumb cluck! We made love more times than ever for those last five months, and he said I had marvelous, downright MARvelous stamina and the hottest libido, to be rolling around with all three of you. I cried almost every night he wasn't with me. I never saw a tear drop from his eyes . . . about any topic. He never caught on that he was the only one. That June I told him I was pregnant. I didn't show until my fourth month. He was quiet. But I could see he was glad. So, he got his make-believe ticket to ride. 'Ain't no kid of mine . . . . that anyone can prove. Maybe I'll feel like coming back some day and adopt it.' A week later, he was gone. "

Moc spoke first. "So, you never heard anything from him until the stranger showed up?"

"Ha! You think it's Pal, too."

"No, I didn't say that. I mean, you never even said his name until somebody said it could be him. So, are you thinking that, too? And why in hell don't you ask someone to ask him, or, for Christ sake, go find him and see for yourself?"

"Because I'm scared shitless, buddy boy."

"Why do you think he's here?"

"Excuse me?! Whyncha go and ask him?"

Hazel went on. "I took out my lie on you all. All. Even Schlom . . . Sam. More. I love him, he knows that. But I hurt him because I wanted to hurt Pal. Now I'm gonna tell him. "

Moc pointed. "He musta heard you, look."

Sam was in the doorway to the back room, staring at Hazel. Hazel looked back. Sam's eyes dropped to the floor. He stepped forward and slowly slumped toward his mother and into her chest. His arms remained at his side. At first, Hazel just leaned into him, then her arms enveloped him and she pressed her cheek to his. Sam was weeping. She held him for minutes, as the others looked away. She wiped his tears with her cheeks, so no one would notice.

"I talked to him, Mama."

"You spoke to him?"

"No, he talked first, and I didn't say anything. But he asked me about my Mama."

Hazel was trembling, and squeezed tighter to steady herself.

"What did you tell him . . . about me?"

"Nothing. I mean . . . I said, do you know my Mama?"

"He said, "Kind of. Does she gather up her hair in back and wrap a rubber band around it when she does the dishes?"

"I looked up at him. I said, so, you seen her?"

"He said, in my mind."

"But, how come you know that?"

Hazel loosened her grip and leaned back just enough to look into Sam's eyes. "What was his answer?"

"He just smiled. He's real tall, so I had to look way up and then he picked me up and I could feel his breath and see his big eyes real close. I said, Scuro says I look like you."

Hazel's eyes closed tight, and she said, trying not to sound anxious, "Good Lord, what did he say to that?"

He kissed me, Mama, and said, "I'm flattered."

I said, "what does that mean?"

"He said, it means Scuro thinks I look good."

Hazel tilted Sam back a bit more to stare into his face. She pushed up his chin to get a full look. Do you understand that? Sam stared into her eyes. She said, "Where did he kiss you?

Sam struggled to pull up his arm which was pressed tight between his chest and Hazel's breast. He pointed to his forehead and then to his mouth. She kissed him hard, first on his mouth, then on his forehead.

Sam just kept looking at her.

"Never mind, that's good, anyway, I mean, it's a nice thing, you know. Did you like him? I mean, do you?"

Sam blinked and flattened his cheek above Hazel's damp bosom.

"Do you?"

"He's nice. He kissed me, like you do, with his mouth and nose. He put me down and hugged me some more. I said, can you come see my

Mama? Can you come and maybe eat at our house?"

"He said, you have to ask your Mama. So, can he, Mama? Can he?"

Hazel sat down. On the gimpy rocking chair. She looked around to find Beal and Moc. It was too quiet. Moc's voice came from the back room, over the sound of the slamming heavy security door. "I saw him. I watched."

Moc was in an uncharacteristic hurry. He walked too quickly toward his chair. Hazel stood up quickly just missing Moc as he sat down hard and tried to rock, banging his heels, on each futile stretch. Hazel felt his tension and held Sam tighter. Sam giggled unexpectedly. She looked into his eyes then pressed her cheek to where Sam said the Man had kissed him.

Moc said, "He's comin' over."

Hazel stared at him. Moc continued, "I saw him talking to Sam."

"What did you hear?" said Hazel.

"I didn't hear much. Your name, a couple times."

"Did you talk to him?"

Moc was tense. "No, why would I wanna talk to him?"

Hazel held Sam tighter. "A lotta questions here today. No answers. Just like always. How do you know he's coming here?"

Moc said, "I followed him over here, only I lost him. Maybe he didn't wanna be followed."

"I don't see any stranger here, do you? So, where'd he go?"

Then she almost gagged. Tears welled up in her eyes so suddenly it blurred her vision, her heart raced so fast it pounded in her ears, and she had to steady herself on the arm of the rocker. She gripped it so tightly that the blood ran out of her head, her brain felt numb and her mouth so dry that she had trouble opening it to breathe.

"Moc, are you telling me true? Did you follow him or did he follow you? Moc! did you do something? Moc! Did you?"

Customers had been strolling in and out. Most picked up and examined a few items, no one bought anything. Hazel was near the cash register, just in case. Squeezing Sam, gradually regaining her breath and her balance, she looked around trying to see Beal. Had he heard all of this, any of it? Had

Moc talked to him? They were both out of sight.

Scuro and Luce came in from the back room. Scuro said, "Well, it's over."

Hazel said, "What's over?"

Luce said, "The awful fight, thank god!"

Hazel was suddenly frozen. She saw Beal and Moc beating the Man. She saw the smaller men ganging up on him. She saw the Man bleeding. She had heard nothing. Until Scuro spoke, all she was aware of was Sam and her racing heart, her parched mouth, damp bosom and blurred vision. And that Beal had been absent for too long. Now Moc was gone, too. When? She couldn't think straight. She tried to speak.

"The Man is here."

Hazel's back was to Moc. She stood motionless. Feeling limp, she reached for the old cash register to steady herself. Her legs barely supported her. Sam clung to her long skirt, slowly, self-consciously wiping his eyes with her apron, conscious of not tugging, so she wouldn't know. Hazel felt comforted by Sam's heated embrace. She leaned into him.

Moc was in the back room doorway. Barely looking up, Hazel saw a shadow half covering Moc's face. He was smiling. But where was Beal?

Then Beal elbowed halfway past Moc. He was smiling, too, although a trickle of blood was visible running to his chin from the corner of his mouth. Moc shifted under Beal's weight. The shadow left his face, and she glimpsed a large bruise on his cheek and jaw.

A large veiny hand floated out of the dark and settled gently on top of Moc's head, seeming to pet it, then swiftly and vigorously rumpled Beal's shaggy locks. Moc smiled sheepishly. Beal grunted and tried to swipe away the hand, but missed, then growled like a dog.

A sweeping laugh flew into the store like a fluttering bird. At first It squawked, then chirped, and softened to a chortle, which strangely grew louder as an extra large arm shoved a thick clenched fist past both men and gripped the inner door frame.

THE MEETING

Oliver - October 1994

When Oliver raised his paws to beg,
My heart gave in to the world.
There was no chance I could renege;
Resistance was unfurled.

Northwest by south he came to me
And crept into our lives
But not until he climbed a tree
And a plan he could contrive

A way to join two snarling beasts
In a household full of hearts
Where his gentle kiss earned daily feasts
And treats of chicken parts.

His self respect drew instant friends;
The dogs knew who he was.
And Kitty tried but couldn't offend,
If challenged, he'd simply pause

He hunted, though, he was no prude
And ate his prey sometimes
And left entrails, but never crude,
He'd never deal in crimes.

On the grass or hearth or tennis deck
He'd ask you with his Aowh!
To rub his droopy belly, his neck
Then hum like a garbage scow.

Oh, Oliver, Oliver! I'm glad you came
To share your life with us.
We'll miss your plaintive flailing game
Send back your succubus.